MW01045527

Before the New Moon Rises

Before the New Moon Rises

Cathy Hird

To Megan
Cathy Hird

Torquere Press Publishers

P.O. Box 37, Waldo, AR 71770.

Before the New Moon Rises by Cathy Hird Copyright 2015

Cover illustration by Kris Norris

Published with permission

www.torquerepress.com

ISBN: 978-1-944449-05-6

PRINT ISBN: 978-1-944449-06-3

First Torquere Press Printing: December 2015

Printed in the USA

Before the New Moon Rises

Cathy Hird

Before the New Moon Rises

Map by Paul Hird and Angela Ritchie

MT OLYMPUS

ACHERON RIVER
EPHYRA
MT PELION

DELPHI • THEBES •

GULF OF CORINTH
CORINTH •
MYCENAE •
TIRYNS

• SPARTA

ANCIENT
GREECE

Prologue

Seventh day after the full moon

The knife sparked as Aphoron slid it along the granite top of the palace guard wall, honing the bronze blade to a killing edge. The rasping sound matched the anger that seethed in his heart, and the knife flashed red as blood in the light of the setting sun. He imagined throwing the blade, cutting Melanion, the prince of Tiryns, who had ruined his plans.

That prince was out of his reach for the moment. Melanion feasted in the palace hall with Aphoron's father, the king of Ephyra. High ranking merchants of the city had been invited to the celebration, but Aphoron was banished from company to prepare for a test he did not plan to accept.

Aphoron threw the knife at the balustrade. It stuck in the wood and quivered there. If only he could cut the interfering prince as easily.

Aphoron retrieved the knife and returned to sharpening it. They had been so close to moving his city out of its farm-centered quagmire. If his father had shifted his allegiance to the Olympian Poseidon, they could have joined the ranks of trading powers—cities like Corinth, Sparta, and Athens. Instead the old goddess had shown up, and his father had turned away from the power of Olympus. The king had bowed once more to the Mother Goddess Eurynome, and her only interest was dirt and growing things. Thanks to her interference, life in the valley of Ephyra was all barley and olives again.

I'll make that prince pay! Aphoron threw the knife again. The goddess had convinced his father to promote his younger half-brother until Aphoron showed he could be trusted. Then, she had dared to set him a task, a test of his allegiance. She had the nerve to tell him to go north to Corfu to hunt a monster shark that tormented fishing folk there.

He pulled the knife from the wood. "I am not going on a random quest just because an old goddess tells me to."

"Then make your own choice."

Aphoron turned sharply and raised his knife. Poseidon, God of Ocean and Earthshaking, leaned on the wall gazing across the valley.

"Sharp as it is, that knife would not hurt me." Poseidon spoke quietly, but his voice was cold as the depths of the ocean.

Aphoron glared but lowered the knife. "What are you doing back in our city? The goddess Eurynome banished you."

"Do not mention that hag." Poseidon clenched his fist and brought it down hard on top of the waist high wall. The granite shook. Then, he opened his hands and laid his palms on the stone. "I have an opportunity for you."

"The last opportunity you offered turned as sour as milk left in the sun. Why should I listen when Eurynome and her minions defeated you?"

"Careful, young prince. Show proper respect, and I may show you a path to revenge and renewed power."

"Revenge?" The word tasted sweet on Aphoron's tongue. The idea that he could regain power made his heart pound. He sheathed the knife.

"You can let the hag lead you by the nose, or choose your own hunt, a new path where you shape your own future." The god never looked away from the distant hills. "A son of mine, one of the tribe of Cyclopes, helped build the walls of Tiryns. He keeps a secret that could open an opportunity for you."

Aphoron studied the profile of the god. His father had granted him only three ships for the hunt in Corfu, not enough for an assault on the city of the offending prince. Yet, if this son of Poseidon knew of a secret weakness, there might be a way. "What do you want me to do?"

"Do what you want." Poseidon still gazed at the distant mountains. "If you do not act, your brother will be king.

Based on his marriage to that delicate young princess, your father will see an opportunity for an alliance with Tiryns, city of the prince you hate. You will lose everything." He turned and seemed to study Aphoron. "On the other hand, I can open a path for you to take it all back."

A smile slowly came to Aphoron's lips. "Where do I find your son?"

the goddess had caused it to shine red as a harvest moon, though it was early spring. She sighed. "I had so hoped for the peace the goddess promised."

"That peace will come." Panacea turned to the younger woman. "First, there are tasks to be finished. We must not forget the shark that is plaguing Corfu. And Poseidon, like most Olympians, works in threes. You too may have work to do."

Melanion frowned. "I trust you will be safe here at the shrine, but given this time of turmoil, I will assign a guard to stay near you."

Thalassai stood and looked her brother in the eyes. She could be strong. "Such a soldier will be an honor guard, I am certain. Do not fear for me. I'll stay to build our new alliance with this city and the people who serve the goddess," said Thalassai. "I do hate to see you riding into danger, though."

"It'd be more dangerous to leave that pig Aphoron free to do what he wants," said Dermios.

***

Waves gently lapped the shore as the four horses pounded across the beach. Their shadows stretched almost to the base of the hills as the sun fell toward the horizon. Small rocky islands dotted the calm blue water but there were no ships. The only boats they had seen all day were small fishing skiffs. No sign of the larger transports with their oars and white sail. The empty sea worried Melanion. *Where is Aphoron?* he wondered.

He glanced over his shoulder. Dermios and Panacea were right behind. The soldier from Ephyra, the one who would carry a message back to the king, rode a horse's length behind them. The man's face was set in a frown, and he looked uncomfortable.

Melanion turned back to study the terrain and find where their path would climb back up the forested slope. His thoughts remained focused on the soldier. He wondered if the man was unaccustomed to riding at speed or if he was uneasy about this assignment. He hoped the king had

chosen the messenger wisely. After all, three shiploads of
sailors had disobeyed the king and followed Aphoron. There
would be a problem if this man supported the disgraced
prince. *He must carry a true message back when we learn where
Aphoron has gone.*

Melanion led his companions up the hill and into the pine
forest. In the cooler air, he leaned forward to rub the neck
of his stallion. Even without a full day's rest in Ephyra, the
horse accepted another hard ride. He heard the sound of
falling water, saw a stream that crossed the path. The stallion
blew quietly. "You're right," Melanion said to his horse, "a
drink is in order." He raised a hand to signal a halt. "We'll
refill our water skins."

"I believe that we are nearing the gulf," said the Ephyran
soldier. "The mountain there produces many streams."

Panacea slipped off her white mare. "Dermios will
probably tell us that someone placed this stream here just to
refresh us." She glanced back at the man still sitting astride
his chestnut stallion. She frowned. "Dermios?"

Melanion turned to study his companion. *Why doesn't he
dismount?* Dermios would be as thirsty as any of them. The
scar that cut across his eyebrow looked white against his
tanned skin. "You hear something in the trees?"

"The mountain provides the very best water." Dermios
gazed at the waterfall. "It tastes like no other, and it brings
good health to all who drink from it."

"Well, let me taste and see what special properties it
has." Panacea knelt, cupped her hands, and reached into the
falling stream.

"You know this place?" asked Melanion, still watching his
companion.

"Never been here." Dermios slid from his horse and let
the chestnut drink from the pool.

"That sounds more like you," Melanion said, and then he
met his companion's eyes and saw pain written across his
face. "You know something about this mountain, though."

"My home village was on its south-facing slope. We
mined copper there." Dermios gazed upward. "Tomorrow, if
we keep riding along the coast, we will pass below the place

among crafters' shops and houses sounded wonderful. She would be able to change out of these working clothes and dress more like a princess. Then, she made her face serious. She hoped that her relief at the offer of escape did not show too clearly. "I want to learn everything about Ephyra." She looked toward the shrine. "Here comes the high priestess now."

"Prince Brizo," Asira said, "you are welcome to the home of the goddess." She placed a hand on her heart and bowed to him. "Is there something in particular you wish from the Mother?"

"I came with one request, and now would ask a second favor. My father wishes to know what you have heard about the far corners of our valley. And I seek Thalassai's company for the afternoon to walk in the city with me. She has not seen much of Ephyra."

"If she desires this," said Asira, "I will place her in your care for this day."

Thalassai bristled "Surely, I am free to choose where I go."

"You are not restricted by us, but the king expects a certain decorum from the royal family," said Asira, "and your brother assigned a bodyguard for your honor and security."

Thalassai blushed. She had overreacted. Protocol was important. It limited freedom, but it was very different than captivity. This was a city she did not know, and even at home she would not walk out alone. Still, being handed to another's care pricked her pride. "It seems to me that in a city recovering from the threat of disaster, the citizens are reassured when the people of the palace walk among them."

The priestess met her eyes with a solemn gaze. "It is good for the people to see a representative of the shrine as well. Eurynome blessed you, and the people will sense her blessing when you walk among them."

Thalassai blushed again. Her role in this city was complex. *I guess I need her guidance and Brizo's too.*

Brizo sensed her discomfort and changed the subject. "The river continues to rise?"

"Two handspans in two days. The nearby irrigation channels are flowing, and soon, the water will flow again to the far reaches of the valley. The farmers begin to relax. They trust the Mother to care for them once more."

"Then we can hope for a strong harvest," said Brizo.

"That is what the Mother promised. It is good to feel the hope of our people. Sadly that is not the spirit among the people of Corfu," said Asira. "They are still in danger from the beast Mother Eurynome sent Aphoron to slay. Do we know yet whether he accepted the task the Mother gave him?"

"The messenger who went south with Melanion has not returned," said Brizo. "First indications were not good, but the king is not ready to assume that Aphoron has betrayed his trust."

Thalassai glanced over at Brizo. She heard a note of bitterness when he spoke of his half-brother. It bothered Brizo that his father could not see Aphoron's true nature. She agreed with him that the prince had shown his greed and ambition clearly enough. She did not trust him at all, though she acknowledged that her bias ran as deep as the waters of the ocean.

"We will face that concern when the messenger returns," said Asira. "But for today, the task is light: show this princess the strength and beauty of your city."

Thalassai felt her shoulders lift. She would enjoy this visit to the hill that stood on the other side of the river. "It will not take me long to wash and change," she said to Brizo.

"Come Brizo; look over the land while you wait," said Asira. "See for yourself that the green returns."

In the room that had been assigned to her, Thalassai found an urn filled with warm water for washing. She really should not complain about the work she had to do. The people of the shrine looked after her needs, treated her as an honored guest.

Thalassai washed the dirt from her forehead and scrubbed her hands as best she could. Evidence that she had been working in the garden remained around her nails, but she could not remove the dirt that had been pressed into the crevices. She cast aside the short robe and put on a linen one that Asira had provided. The spiral clips for the shoulders were made of copper, and the green robe hung to her ankles. Dressed this way, she felt much more like herself.

As she combed her hair smooth, Thalassai was thankful she had learned to do this task during her captivity. She redid the braid and placed the only bracelet she had on her arm, and then slid her feet into her leather sandals. She wished she had a necklace and an armband, but she was not going to a feast or a palace event. It was just a walk in the city. She stood tall, as her father would expect, and headed out to enjoy the company of the prince.

Chapter Three

Ninth day after the full moon

The sun had risen a handspan above the waters of the gulf
when Melanion and his companions rode into a narrow cove
with a cluster of huts built back against the forest edge. Not
a person was in sight. Melanion pulled his stallion to a halt.
Dermios slipped from his horse.

"Where is everyone?" Panacea asked.

Melanion dismounted. Goats were tethered in the shade,
and a carefully laid out garden flourished near the small
stream that ran across the cove toward the ocean. The people
who tended this quiet place must be nearby.

A squawking chicken ran from the trees, and a child
chased it between the huts. He caught the hen and held it
tight. He stood, legs apart, and faced Melanion. He squared
his shoulders and set his mouth in a defiant look.

Melanion tried not to smile at the courage of the child.
"You cannot live here alone with your hen."

"He does not." An old woman walked from the forest and
stood behind the boy. She put her hands on his shoulders.
"Tell me what we must give you, then be on your way."

"We seek nothing from you," said Panacea. "You need not
fear us."

Dermios dropped the reins of his stallion. "Salanta, you're
alive!"

The old woman looked past Panacea and Melanion. Her
eyes opened in surprise. "Dermios? Is this truly Dermios,
son of our chief and headwoman?"

Dermios stepped forward. He laid a tentative hand on the
woman's shoulder. She embraced him, held him with tears

running down her cheeks. The child looked up with wonder and confusion in his eyes.

"What are you doing here?" Dermios asked. "Where are the others?"

"There are more of you, I take it." Melanion scanned the edge of the forest but saw no sign of anyone else.

Salanta released her tight hold on Dermios, but kept a hand on each of his shoulders. "Come!" she called. "It's not the *Others*. It's Dermios! One of the *Taken* returns."

Dermios touched her cheek lightly. "What are you doing here by the ocean? How many survived?"

"You have not come to raid us?" The boy held the hen tightly as he stared up at Dermios.

Dermios smiled, but his hand shook as he laid it gently on the boy's shoulder. "You are a courageous young man," he said, "running out to save this little one."

Eyes wide with amazement, tears glistening in their corners, he studied the collection of women and children who came from their hiding places among the trees. They crowded as close to Dermios as they could get. He hugged a teenage boy, a cousin who had been too young for the slavers to bother with, placed a hand on the arm of his aunt. He hugged his father's sister and her two daughters. "I am astonished to find you."

"This was your village?" Panacea asked.

"These are my people." Dermios kept scanning the faces around him. "The village was much higher up the mountain."

"We who remained were not strong enough to keep mining," said Salanta. "We moved here where we could fish, and planting gardens was easier. We never expected any of you to return." She paused, looked Dermios in the eyes. "Do you know what happened to the others?"

"We were sold at the slave market in Athens. My cousin Cephano serves in the court of the king there. I do not know where the others went."

"I always wondered what your interest in the serving man was." Melanion studied Dermios. "You would never say."

"There was no point." Dermios took a deep breath, and his voice broke when he spoke. "My mother?"

"I am sorry, Dermios. She died two winters ago. She was a strong leader until then."

The smile left Dermios' mouth and eyes. Melanion laid a hand on his shoulder, felt a shudder go through him. "I did not believe I would see any of you again," Dermios said slowly, "but still I imagined her living somewhere beyond my reach."

Salanta touched his cheek, and her voice was thick with sadness. "As we hoped you lived, prayed that you were well in that foreign land." She turned to Melanion and Panacea. "If you are friends of this son of our village, you are welcome, though we have little to offer you today."

"What happened this morning?" asked Panacea. "Something frightened you."

"Just after dawn, raiders came from the sea. They took the fish we had smoked, all our bread, the roots we had gathered. We are thankful they took none of us, but we are now short of food."

"How many ships?" Melanion's voice was hard as a bronze blade.

"Three," said Salanta. "They flew no flags, but their accents were northern. One grabbed young Dalia here, but the leader said they were in a hurry, no time to play. I would have torn the skin from their bones if they hurt one of our girls."

"Aphoron." Melanion looked out to the water wishing he had been here sooner. If only they had ridden faster, caught up with the disgraced prince here. Melanion folded his arms, told himself that wishing did no good.

"Pig!" Dermios pounded his fist into his palm. "Brute of a bear! How could he treat my people so?"

"You're lucky he didn't know they were your people," said Panacea, "or they might have fared worse."

"We would feast your return, but we have no food. We must organize a group to gather greens and roots, and another to fish. You'll stay so that we can arrange a celebration?"

"I cannot stay for a feast," Melanion said. *But I can undo this deed.* He turned to Salanta. "We will hunt and fish for you this morning." He reached into the pouch that hung by his scabbard on the stallion. "This amber will buy you grain for flour. It does not repay the time I've kept this son of your village away from you, but it will help with what was taken today."

"What Aphoron's men did is not your fault." Dermios put his hand on the shoulder of one of the younger children.

"This prince of Ephyra has become my responsibility," Melanion said. "Anger at me is part of what drives him. We'll do what we can to repair the damage he did here."

"Truly, you'll delay our chase, for the sake of my people?" Dermios kept his hand on the child's shoulder, but his other hand clenched into a fist and unclenched again.

Melanion's lips lifted into a smile that did not touch his eyes. "Half a day and then I must go, attempt to prevent more destruction by this rogue prince. If you chose to stay here…"

"I'll not stay behind. For now." Dermios turned Salanta. "I'll return when this quest is accomplished, help with whatever work needs doing."

"I will come with you when you return." Melanion surveyed the group. "Panacea, if you would, tend to any who are ill. I will hunt, and Dermios can lead a fishing crew. Then, we will chase down Aphoron and make him pay one more score."

Chapter Four

Ninth day after the full moon

With Brizo at her side and guards in front, Thalassai strolled down the grassy slope that led from the shrine to the wide river. They crossed the slow flowing water on a swinging bridge made of wooden planks. On the far shore, a cluster of houses stood between the river and the base of the hill, twin to the one the shrine was built on, but covered with gray stone buildings. She knew that near the top of the hill, the houses were larger and had gardens. Here at its base they were built almost on top of each other.

To the west, Thalassai could see the shining waters of the sheltered port, and she knew that a wide avenue led down to that busy shore. Here, the path was only wide enough for two to walk side by side as they wound their way upward. From time to time, narrow stone stairs climbed to the next level.

A group of women carrying baskets bowed to Brizo and Thalassai, and Thalassai nodded to them. As they climbed slowly toward the farm market, she listened to Brizo describe the organization of the city, where the forges of the smiths clustered near the base of the hill, where the potters' quarter could be found.

"In Tiryns, the smiths are all located near the outside wall that protects the city," said Thalassai. "It's different in Corinth and Sparta, where the trades are clustered around the temples dedicated to the god or goddess who is their patron."

"You have traveled a great deal. I know only this coast."

Thalassai thought Brizo pulled away a little. Perhaps he was intimidated by her experience. "You visited the south with your brother when…" She swallowed, not wanting to refer directly to her kidnapping.

"My brother assigned me to guard the ship in each port. He did not trust me." Brizo shrugged. "He sensed my disagreement with the plan from the beginning, I suppose."

"So you did not see the beauty of my city, its palace and the three well-crafted temples."

"I admired the massive stone walls from the vantage point of the port," said Brizo. "There are temples inside your city?"

"Indeed. We have long had temples for Athena and Aphrodite. A new one for Poseidon was just completed. Because we rely on trade by ship, Father wanted to curry the god's favor."

"That did not work out very well," said Brizo.

Thalassai shivered at the memory of the god's cold touch when he came to claim her. "The sailors are happy to have a place to offer prayers before their voyages. I went to the consecration ceremony but no other time. I prefer Athena's temple."

"And these shrines are within the city walls." Brizo shook his head. "I am too used to our system with the shrine separate from the city, a partner with the palace in the care of the valley." He walked in silence for a moment, brow creased. "I have assumed our way was the only way. I would like to visit your city." He smiled, and this time it reached his eyes. "And not just the port."

"I would be glad to show you my home. The palace is beautiful, and the gardens are a wonder. We have plants from all over the south, and herbs that my brother brought home from Mount Pelion."

"I hope you will come to call this city home." Brizo touched her arm lightly.

Thalassai studied his face. The expression was quiet, reserved. Only the lines by his eyes revealed his sense of humor, and they appeared too seldom. For too long he had held back his thoughts, kept himself in his half-brother's shadow. Perhaps that was part of the attraction for her. So many of the sons of southern rulers were brash and over-confident.

"The market is just ahead." Brizo pointed up a short, steep flight of stairs. "Here, we meet the farmers who are the foundation of our valley."

With the two soldiers in the lead and her guard behind, they entered an open plaza crowded with people. The air was sweet with the fresh scent of berries. The chatter sounded cheerful as people of the city examined the produce displayed in baskets or set out on rugs. Thalassai saw lettuce, spinach, and early scallions, bushels of grain from the previous fall's harvest.

"Greetings, Prince and Princess," said an old woman with berries to sell. "Will you sample my produce?"

"The palace cook trusts only his chosen assistant to make purchases," said Brizo, "but I will tell him that yours look to be a marvel."

"And someone from the shrine will come later today. I am sure they will consider your berries," said Thalassai.

"Aye, Asira herself was here the day you arrived. We spoke of the river. Tell her the new berries are larger, the way they ought to be. The water is returning. Thanks be to the goddess and to you, Princess."

"It was my brother who found the crack under the mountain that bled away the water of the river." *I trust his current path is nowhere near as dark,* Thalassai thought.

"I saw you stand tall before the Earthshaker. Your courage opened space for the miracle the goddess wrought." The woman lifted a few of the berries from her basket and laid them on Thalassai's palm. "A small token of thanks."

Thalassai placed the berries on her tongue. The juice refreshed her mouth, and the rich sweetness surprised her. "They are wondrous."

Three soldiers marched into the square. "Prince Brizo!" one shouted. "King Kratos summons you to his presence. Immediately. The presence of Princess Thalassai is also required."

Silence fell in the square as buyers and sellers looked from the soldiers to Brizo and Thalassai. She glanced at Brizo. He pressed his lips into a tiny smile, but his brow furrowed. She could feel tension in his whole body. The smile was for the public.

Her own guard stepped up beside her. "Must you heed this command?" he asked quietly so that only she and Brizo heard.

"What my father commands must be." Brizo met her eyes briefly, took a deep breath, then opened his hands and spread his arms wide. He raised his voice to speak to all in the market. "It is a shame that the princess and I will not have a chance to examine all your wares. I carry your news to the king: the waters return! Thanks be to Mother Eurynome for blessing our valley once again."

With a slow, gracious sweep of his arm, Brizo invited Thalassai to follow the soldiers across the square. She examined his face, read concern in his eyes but no other clue. He was right that they had no choice; no one could disregard such a public demand. They crossed the square and followed the soldiers up a narrow alley. Her own guard was tense and walked barely half a step behind her.

Thalassai pasted a smile to her lips. She walked as gracefully as she could, thinking that her father would not use such a public display of authority. He simply expected his people, including his family, to trust his instructions.

Thalassai did not trust this king. Summoning Brizo was one thing: if there was news about Aphoron, he should be among the first to hear it. But he had summoned her as well. Perhaps Melanion had sent a message back to her. Her mind raced to wild possibilities. "What do you…" Thalassai started to ask.

"In a moment," Brizo whispered then he smiled brightly to the knot of people walking toward them. When they passed, he said, "I do not know what troubles my father, but my guess is that the messenger who went south with your brother has returned. I believe we will soon discover where my half-brother headed."

"It will be good to hear from my brother," said Thalassai.

"I doubt it." Brizo must have noticed the way she

stiffened. He softened his voice. "I know you meant it will be good to have some questions answered, but I am concerned about Aphoron's intentions. I do not believe the news will be good."

"I too am concerned," said Thalassai, "but I have come to feel that the knife-edge of waiting is the hardest."

Brizo gave her a half-smile. "Sometimes what comes after the waiting is the true challenge."

"But you engage it." Thalassai bit her lower lip. "When I actually faced your father on the beach, I dug up the strength to speak. Talking with you the day before, I could not imagine how I could handle what was coming."

They came to the gate in the palace wall. The lintel above it was carved with four coiled snakes. Poseidon's servant had not been able to remove these symbols of the mother goddess, although he had burned the ancient oak in the courtyard and planted a plane tree in its place. When they passed into the courtyard, Thalassai saw that the tree chosen by the Olympian was gone. A seedling oak had been planted where the ancient tree once stood.

Poseidon's influence had tainted this palace, but the goddess was again its foundation, thanks to the work of her brother and his companions. And thanks to her own strength. Thalassai straightened her shoulders and lifted her chin. The goddess who had supported her in her captivity would stand by her now whatever came next.

Crossing the courtyard, Thalassai slowed her pace. Her father always said that a stately walk looked more confident. Brizo slowed to stay beside her, and she wondered if he understood her need to appear strong. She glanced up and saw that he held his shoulders carefully back. She nodded to herself. He too needed to look calm, though she knew he was uncertain what his father would do with the news of his brother. They climbed the stairs together and entered the throne room side by side.

The king paced the dais at the end of the hall with his hands behind his back and his eyes on the floor. Thalassai looked past him to the fresco painted on the wall, showing the birthplace of the river. In the bright morning light the

sign that whoever was there had noticed their approach.

Melanion tapped a foot silently, waiting, wondering. Two whistles of a dove, and he shrugged. "I don't know who is ahead, but that signal says Dermios sees no danger." He led the two horses along the path with Panacea and her mare following.

A deep growling voice penetrated the thick underbrush. "Company! Twice in one day! How am I to get any work done?"

As Melanion stepped from the forest, a cloud of steam rose from an urn set beside the white-hot coals of a fire. A man with a chest broad as an ox held tongs that he lifted from the water. He examined a sizzling blade of bronze. Dermios stood near him with a bemused smile on his face.

"What miracle have you come for?" The man took a limping step and placed the bronze deep in the fire. "Are you here for a plow that will cut through stone or a sword that will protect from a gorgon? Strange, that request. Swordsmen come seeking a weapon that won't break, but do they take time to study the art of sword work or to practice with a hero like Herakles?" The man pulled the bronze from the fire, placed it on the anvil, and swung his hammer twice.

"When I spent time studying on Mount Pelion," Melanion said, "the eldest centaur Cheiron honed my skill with the sword. He taught me some patience, said I needed more." Melanion turned to hand the reins of the two stallions to Panacea.

"Hephaestus," she said quietly.

Melanion's frown deepened. *What is an Olympian doing on our road?* He turned back to the god, who still examined the bronze he worked. "What is the God of the Forge doing in this land?"

"Poseidon wanted to know the same thing." Hephaestus threw his hammer to the ground, but placed the bronze carefully on the anvil. "You use the tools but don't know where the metal they are forged with comes from." He placed both fists on his hips.

"The best copper comes from the mountain a half day behind us," said Dermios, "and tin from the hills just north of here. This does seem an excellent place for a forge."

"A miner traveling with a supposedly skilled swordsman." Hephaestus studied Dermios. "Interesting, but not enough reason for you to judge my choice."

"What was Poseidon doing here?" Melanion asked.

"I asked myself that question." The god folded his arms. "And it cannot be an accident that you come the same day he did, the same day ships arrived at the island where a cyclops, a son of Poseidon, lives."

"Three ships?" Melanion asked.

"Three boatloads of sailors welcomed by Poseidon's vicious son. Now, on your way."

The tent flap opened, and a woman stepped out. "I heard voices, Hephaestus. We have more company?" Her voice was clear as a silver bell and her form lithe.

"They are leaving," said the Smith.

"You are sending away the daughter of the God of Healing? And a prince of Tiryns?" The woman smiled. "I am Talia, and I invite you to spend the night with us."

The Smith examined Panacea. "You do have your father's eyes and chin. I admire his work, though he doesn't like me much. Blames me for the injuries my tools cause." He turned to Melanion. "I suppose I am done with work for this day. After two interruptions, I will make a mistake." The god shook his head. "Stay the night if you must."

"I will look to the horses," said Panacea. "Where can I find fresh water?"

"Come, and I will take you to the stream." Talia laid a gentle hand on the mare's muzzle. "She is a beauty."

"With horses to admire, it will be a while until we eat." Hephaestus put down his tongs and stirred the fire, separating the coals. "Perhaps you wish to study the ships on the island while I put the fire to rest."

Melanion took a deep breath. He did not need to rush on. Could not, in fact. If they had caught up with Aphoron, he would have to wait to see which way the Ephyrans sailed in the morning. "The sailors may be of interest to me."

"Of course they are of interest to you. I do wonder, however, what connects them and Poseidon and you."

Hephaestus stirred the coals again.

"I crossed the Earthshaker defending my sister," said Melanion. "He is not pleased with me."

Hephaestus laughed sharply. "Well, that is a good thing in my opinion. If you spin a good tale this night I may not be sorry Talia invited you to stay."

"Where can I see this island," asked Melanion, "and the ships that stopped there?"

"Straight through the trees you'll find a rock overhang with a good view, or follow the valley to the sandy cove where Talia likes to go. It was from there that she saw them arrive just after Poseidon visited me. Go. Let me put the fire to rest. Then, I will find the wine that came as payment from the king of Corinth and hear the story of how you disturbed Poseidon's plans."

***

Talia fed them well. When she provided fruit to finish their meal, Hephaestus' mood shifted. He picked up the knife he had been working on when they arrived.

"It is strange to me that some cannot hold on to memory," said the God of the Forge. "Mine is like the metal I work with: the heat of emotion gives it a shape that it will hold forever." The blade flashed in the firelight. "Poseidon's memory is like the ocean, always moving and shifting. He arrived today expecting I would welcome his visit like that of a dear uncle. But I will never forget that he led the laughter when I demonstrated my first wife Aphrodite's infidelity with Ares." Hephaestus looked up and met Melanion's eyes. "So did you learn anything from my rocky ledge?"

"I saw the ships pulled up on the beach of the island, but there was no clue to what Aphoron and his men are doing there." Melanion's mind sifted the possibilities, but he could think of no answer to the question at the top of his mind. "What reason could Poseidon have for drawing them to the island?"

"He did not share his intention. I might guess he gave his

son the giant specific instructions. The brute would rather eat people than eat with them — yet when Talia saw those ships pull onto shore, the giant welcomed the sailors. Soon after, cooking fires were lit, and men were not the meal."

"Aphoron with another of Poseidon's sons," Dermios said. "This cannot be a good thing."

"The Earthshaker is plotting revenge," said Panacea.

"Anger, he tends to remember," said Hephaestus.

"We were not the only ones who got in his way, but we did play a part." Melanion stared at the fire, turned over the possibilities in his mind. A thought occurred to him and he clenched his fists. "He may yet turn his anger against my city. That, Aphoron would enjoy. If only we could reach the island and learn what they plan."

"Your horses cannot swim that far in these waters," said Talia. "As the moon will rise small and not until much later, she will not provide light enough for sailing. Perhaps morning will tell you more, but for tonight you must endure our hospitality."

"And in exchange you will share the full tale of how you disrupted Poseidon's plot," said Hephaestus. "Make the story worth my while."

Chapter Six

Tenth day after the full moon

Fear tightened like a band around her chest when Thalassai woke in total darkness. She felt the motion of a boat at anchor. She tried to call for help, but no sound came from her mouth. Again, she had been kidnapped!

Thalassai forced her eyes open. The white curve of the moon shone through the window of her room at the shrine. *Another nightmare.* She drew in a long, careful breath and let it out just as slowly. There was no light burning in the room as there would have been back at home, but the goddess had broken the darkness with the gift of moonlight.

How often would this dream haunt her? "Every time I am uneasy, I suppose," she whispered aloud. Her voice seemed hollow to her ears. *Which of my choices disturbs my peace this night?* she wondered. Did doubt rise from her choice to move to the palace, or was she simply afraid for Brizo and the dangerous hunt he would embark upon with the dawn?

Thalassai wished there was someone she could talk to about her worries. In Tiryns, there had been her girl cousins, one slightly older and one a little younger, along with a few friends among the daughters of the elite of the city. And always she could pour out her heart to the faithful servant who had cared for her since her mother's death. That servant would be torn apart by horses before revealing any of Thalassai's secrets. She longed for home, or at least someone from home. Perhaps she could send a message summoning her servant north.

Such a message home would have to wait. The fleet had left to follow Melanion the morning before. The one ship that remained must stay in Ephyra as her guard by Melanion's orders. She did not think this a necessary precaution, but she could not override her brother's order.

Thalassai watched until the bright horn of the moon rose out of sight. Dawn would come soon, and day would claim an effort from her. She should sleep. *But no dreams please, Mother Eurynome.* She did not know if the goddess could influence her sleep, so she pictured the garden of the palace in Tiryns, imagined walking through it with her two brothers, laughing in the sun. Soon, she drifted into a quiet darkness.

***

"Selene will accompany you today," said Asira. "She also wishes to visit the river's birthplace."

"I will be glad of the company of one who aided my brother's rescue mission," Thalassai said. "Does she know the way?"

"No. Metia, one of the young girls who lives here, will guide you both. Her home shelters under the Boundary Mountains near that place."

"First, I must go to the shore to honor Brizo as he departs on this hunt," Thalassai insisted.

"Of course. Guards from the king will be here shortly to escort you. Selene and Metia will wait at this side of the bridge until they escort you back."

"I have to take the soldiers to the gate as well?" Thalassai wondered how she would find the peace to seek answers from the goddess with such a crowd around her.

"Your appointed guard from Tiryns will be sufficient," said Asira, "though it would be gracious to take along any who wish to accompany you to the holy place. Others desire the goddess' intercession as you do."

Thalassai blushed. "I know this. Even among the kidnappers, there were a few besides Brizo who did not wish to abandon Eurynome."

"Not all abandoned the Mother, but…." Asira shook her head sadly and looked beyond Thalassai toward the other hill and the city of Ephyra. "Three shiploads of soldiers followed Aphoron away from the task the king and goddess assigned. Some are still tempted to wander like those stars that choose a meandering course through the heavens."

"So it would help for me to encourage those who are constant." Thalassai sighed. "I suppose I could bring any who wish to show their faithfulness on this pilgrimage."

Asira laid a light hand on her shoulder. "The choice to visit the gate before entering the palace is a good one. The people will see that you honor the Mother. Each choice you make establishes how you are thought of in this land. There are no private decisions."

"There never were. I have always been a princess."

"But you expected your brother to rule, and your father's aura shaped how you were seen in your home city," Asira said. "Here, you are a newcomer, but one who helped restore the river. The sight of you walking through the farms will be a comfort to our people, especially with both princes away."

"One my brother chases, and one leaves to chase a monster." Fear tightened Thalassai's throat, but she lifted her chin so it would not show. "Two dangerous hunts. I pray the Mother watches over both."

"Two hunts we see." Asira looked east, toward the mountains that stood high against the eastern sky. Beyond them was the broad plain of Thessaly, and far beyond that, Mount Olympus. "The Olympians say there are three Fates. The Mother always works in fours."

"You think an Olympian is behind the shark in Corfu? Poseidon again?" Thalassai shivered.

"I do not know, but it is possible that he seeks the allegiance of others here in the west, not just Ephyra."

Her bodyguard approached. "The honor guard arrives, Princess."

Thalassai looked over at the gate and saw four soldiers with scarlet cloaks draped over one shoulder. They were dressed more formally than the ones who summoned her and Brizo the day before. She supposed that was because the king also would attend this send off. At least their cloaks

45

were pinned with silver snakes, Eurynome's symbol. "I am ready." *Just words! I feel less ready now.* Still, she was not going to Corfu. She would not have to face Poseidon or any of the plots he had set in motion.

"One more thing." Asira motioned for a girl to approach. She carried a carved olive-wood box. "As you send the prince on his hunt, I thought you might wear this." Asira opened the box and revealed a long silver chain made of four strands braided together. It sparkled in the bright sun. Asira lifted the chain and gently laid it around Thalassai's neck. "At this public and formal event, it is good for you to look like the princess you are. Della will wait to receive it back when you return."

"Thank you." Thalassai touched the beautiful necklace. It felt warm on her neck. She met the priestess' eyes and felt the strength of the goddess in Asira. She sensed the presence of Eurynome like a gentle touch of wind lifting her hair.

Thalassai raised her chin and pressed her shoulders back the way she had seen her father do when he had to attend a difficult meeting. Deep inside, she knew how to do this. "Thank you, Asira, for your hospitality these last two days." A sudden idea came to her. "In a few days, I will return to the shrine to assist here in any way I can." *I've just committed myself to weeding.* She thought she saw approval in the priestess' eyes.

"May the goddess watch your every step and heed the prayers of your heart," said Asira.

Thalassai held herself to a slow regal pace as she crossed to the gate where the honor guard waited. She felt as if everyone in the shrine watched her go.

***

As Thalassai stepped onto the sand of the port-lands, she made herself walk slowly, proudly. Her previous visit to this place had been tumultuous, focused on the king and his plans. This day, she took time to examine the sheltered bay where the river entered the ocean. Small fishing boats were preparing to launch for the day, and those folk stopped to stare at her and her escort. Two trading vessels were pulled up into cradles, and some of the workers who loaded them nudged each other and pointed her way. Just past them sat the ship of her own city, and the captain of that boat strode across the sand toward her. Near where the river joined the ocean, two boats swarmed with sailors loading spears, quivers of arrows and rope. These were the ones Brizo would lead on his hunt.

The ocean awaited all these ships. Thalassai looked out over the rippling, sapphire blue water. Small outcroppings of rock with grass and pine trees growing on them dotted the bay, and she could see the shadow of a large island many ship-lengths out. To the north, at the end of a gentle curve of sand, rose a tall rocky hill that stood like a sentinel. Soon, Brizo would set out on this gentle-looking sea and head past the sentinel rock.

Deep furrows crossed her brow. She was staying in Ephyra because of Brizo, but this day she had come to bid him farewell. The paths of life never seemed to lead in a straight line. At least she could carry her questions and her doubts to the goddess at the river's gate.

The captain from Tiryns bowed to her with both hands on his heart. "You fare well, Princess? Is the guard assigned you adequate for your needs?"

"Arrangements are more than adequate." Thalassai nodded slightly. "Have you and your men been cared for?"

"Too well. We'll be weary with boredom in a day or two."

Thalassai tilted her head slightly. "Perhaps you could arrange a practice session with the local soldiers. My brother Melanion says there is always more to learn, and strangers are the best teachers."

"A good idea." The captain looked out over the water. "I have planned an exploration of this bay as well. Good to learn the ways of the winds on this coast. For today, the men are checking ropes and planking."

Brizo came down the ladder of one of his ships and walked toward them. The prince took her hand and bowed. Thalassai laid a hand on his shoulder. "May the goddess keep you safe on this hunt and bring you back to me, and to your people, in haste."

Brizo smiled slightly. "Patience is called for even when we hope for haste. Thank you for the prayer, however." He turned to the captain. "You will watch over your princess, I trust."

At that moment, one of the sailors hurried across the sand. "Brizo, I do not think we need the barrels of water you ordered loaded. The weight will slow us down."

Thalassai saw the smile disappear from Brizo's face. She frowned at this newcomer and his challenge to the prince's authority.

The captain from her city spoke up. "Carrying extra water is a brilliant safeguard, Prince Brizo." He emphasized the title. "We always assume that we will be able to land, find water, but the beast you hunt is just as likely to keep you at sea as force you to land."

The disapproving sailor bristled, but Brizo spoke quietly. "What is loaded is loaded, Apro. We leave as soon as the king comes to commission us."

Horns sounded. Sailors stopped work, and the attention of everyone shifted to the column of soldiers who escorted the king of Ephyra onto the port-lands. King Kratos wore a scarlet robe with silver clasps at the shoulders and a circle of silver on his head. He walked slowly, looking straight ahead. Thalassai touched the chain Asira had provided, asked Eurynome for strength, and made herself stand as tall and regal as she could.

Brizo squeezed her hand, and then stepped forward to kneel before his father. The king laid a hand on his head. Kratos commanded him to rise and then addressed the sailors.

"The Goddess Eurynome has informed us of the plight of our allies on the isle of Corfu. Do you accept this task?"

"Aye!" the sailors cried with one voice.

The king motioned for Thalassai to step forward. "You have seen this lovely princess who traveled to us from far-off Tiryns. Today, I present her as the chosen wife of the prince who leads this hunt."

Cheers erupted among the people, but a knot of

discomfort formed in Thalassai's chest. She had insisted on waiting for her father's permission before formalizing this engagement. Now that the king had preempted that, a refusal from her father would cause offense. She glanced at the captain of the Tiryns' ship, but his face was a mask that revealed nothing.

Brizo stepped forward. "Thank you, Father, for sharing the promise of good fortune in my life." The tone of his voice expressed gratitude, but something closer to anger flared in his eyes. "I am indeed blessed that this beautiful and wise princess of a powerful city has turned admiring eyes upon me. The celebration must wait, however, for her brother's return with the blessing of her father on our union. And a dangerous hunt must be accomplished first." He turned to the fishers, sailors, and merchants who watched. "Pray for victory and our quick return!"

Sailors and city people cried out their prayers to Eurynome. Thalassai heard a couple of voices call on Poseidon to guard him, but she could not be sure who spoke that god's name. She worried that the city had not completely turned back to the Mother, but the knot in her chest released a little. Brizo had acknowledged the need to wait for her father's permission.

Brizo touched her cheek lightly, and then stepped toward the boats. "We head into the waves, my companions. For the good of our city and for Corfu, we hunt!"

He and the other sailors climbed into the boats and settled onto the rowing benches. He gave the signal, and shore workers pushed them from their cradles into the lapping waters of the bay. Brizo called the rhythm for the rowers. Slowly at first, then more swiftly than Thalassai thought possible, the boats pulled away from shore into the deep waters.

King Kratos turned away and headed for the city with his escort. His new steward stepped up beside Thalassai. "Will you come to the palace now?"

Thalassai took a sharp inward breath and pulled her eyes from the ships. Had no one told the steward her plan? "First, I will make a pilgrimage to the river's gate."

"Alone?"

The steward sounded concerned, and Thalassai wondered if he wanted to prevent this or was simply checking that she would be properly escorted. She remembered Asira's suggestion. "Indeed not. You are welcome to accompany me."

"There is urgent work I must return to," said the steward.

"You know best, I am sure. My personal guard will accompany me along with two women from the shrine."

"That should be adequate." The steward turned away.

Something about his manner and tone of voice still bothered Thalassai. "Indeed, but my prayers for Brizo would be strengthened by prayers from the people of his city. And given…" Thalassai could not think of a way to mention the betrayal of Eurynome by the previous steward without insulting this man so new to his position. "I believe it would please the Mother if soldiers from the king came to pray to her."

The steward's eyes narrowed. He pointed to the soldiers who had escorted her from the shrine. "You four accompany the princess and then lead her back to the palace." The linen of his robe snapped as he turned quickly to march after the king.

Thalassai turned back to the gentle blue waters and watched the boats approach the sentinel rock. With each stroke of their oars, Brizo went farther and farther from her.

Thalassai's mind churned. Two men she loved had left this city, Brizo into immediate danger and her brother into the unknown. Her chest hurt. By her own decision, she was going to live with the king who had treated her this day like a silver armband to display to the crowd. She wondered if she should refuse to move to the palace. Despite the work, life at the shrine was much simpler.

She turned and walked back to the river escorted by her bodyguard and the local soldiers. At the river's edge, Thalassai looked back up at the hill and the city. From this vantage point, she could not see the palace at its crest. She did know how to live in a city, how to be a princess. At least she knew how in Tiryns. In this city the conflicts and issues flowed like the tides of an unknown sea. *But the king didn't really give me a choice,* she told herself. *And I'll learn.*

It was good that she first traveled to the river's birthplace. Thalassai needed Eurynome's guidance, her reassurance that she had done right. As she crossed the bridge, she was aware of the river flowing beneath them, waters constantly moving. Life was like that, she knew, movement and change, and maybe that was all that made her uneasy. There had been too much change. *And too much danger. Will Brizo meet the monster before the sun sets?* she wondered.

Thalassai and her guards met Della, Selene, and a young girl in the shelter of the shrine's hill. "The king made this send-off a ceremony, I presume," said Della. She opened the box she carried to receive the silver chain. "Asira was wise to give you something to remind him you have status in and of yourself. He'd best not forget that father of yours."

Thalassai lifted the beautiful braided piece off her neck. It had helped make her feel like a princess and had connected her to the goddess. She felt less regal and less like a part of the shrine community as she took it off.

Della touched Thalassai's cheek gently. "The Mother came to you in your captivity, when you needed her. I have only spoken to her face to face once, the day the former high priestess died. Most days, the land and the water speak for her. Every sound the river makes sings of her."

Thalassai frowned. She wanted to speak to Eurynome, but Della knew the ways of the goddess so much better than she did. Perhaps the Mother would not come, and this would be a wasted trip.

Della smiled gently as if reading her thoughts. "This is a good pilgrimage you are making whether or not you see the Mother herself." Della smiled gently, then turned to the young girl, Metia, who would guide them. "Treat that basket gently. It has eggs for your mother. There is also an herb for your father to treat the goat with the infected udder. Tell him to apply the paste twice each day from now until the new moon."

"They will be so grateful." The girl hugged the basket.

Selene put a light hand on Thalassai's arm. "Thank you

for letting me accompany you today. I have long desired to stand in the holy waters of the river's gate."

Thalassai tried to smile. "Let us go, then." For Metia, this was a visit home, and for Selene it was the fulfillment of a long-held dream. The pilgrimage was a good one for them whether the goddess came to her or not. She sighed. She needed the Mother's assurance, and prayed she would come.

"The cyclops!" Panacea pointed to the lumbering form of the giant exiting the trees to cross the beach. "Someone is walking beside him."

"It is too far to be sure who it is." Melanion squinted, trying to identify the human form.

"Only one of them is fit company for that thing," Dermios said.

"That *thing* is a son of Poseidon," said Panacea, "and all his children are powerful. Think of Pegasus. Beautiful. Strong and fast. Arrogant as his father and ready to knock you off a cliff if you cross him."

"Do you know anything about this cyclops' character?" asked Dermios. "He didn't inherit his father's looks."

Melanion watched the movement of the cyclops. "It was said that the giants who built the walls of Tiryns did so to thank my grandfather for a service he rendered. *That* tribe of Cyclopes showed *honor*."

"No matter what sparked that service, Poseidon's claim supersedes it." Panacea glanced at Melanion, then turned back to the island. "Clearly, the Earthshaker was here ahead of Aphoron."

"What instruction could the god have delivered to his son?" Melanion picked up a rock and threw it as far as he could. It sailed in a long arc into the surf below the cliff. "Where does Aphoron go next?"

"They have to land at Corinth," said Dermios, "if they go east."

"And then what?" asked Panacea.

Melanion watched the ships in silence as the sailors pushed the boats into the water and climbed in. With motions well practiced by men from every city up and down the coast, they began to row toward the east.

"We head for Corinth, it seems." Melanion turned his back on the sea and stalked toward the horses.

Dermios took one last look at the island where the cyclops still stood on the beach before following. "They might stop somewhere along the way."

"There are many small villages on both the northern and southern coasts of this gulf," said Panacea. "If he lands on this shore again, we will deal with him."

"And if he raids someplace on the southern shore? He'll plunder those innocent people the way he did mine."

"That we cannot prevent. I promise I will do all I can to make him pay for any raids." Frustration tightened around Melanion's heart. He worried about the owl's message, the references to Ephyra and kings. The message also mentioned his home, and Tiryns had been unprotected for too long. With the prevailing wind at their back, the fleet should arrive in his city in three days. If he rode directly, he could arrive the same day, but he had no way of knowing where Aphoron's trail would lead.

The next step in that hunt was clear. The Ephyran ships would stop at the Corinthian land-bridge. At that place, guarded by soldiers from Corinth, there would be some evidence of Aphoron's plans, if only what transport he engaged. Melanion laid a hand on his stallion's neck and mounted. One day's journey at a time. "We race for Corinth."

Chapter Eight

Tenth day after the full moon

Two farmers stopped their weeding to study the group walking along the river. Thalassai felt their gaze as an intrusion on her private pilgrimage. She had questions to ask the Mother, desperately needed Eurynome's reassurance. All these people made it hard for her to remain focused.

Thalassai reminded herself that being seen was part of the purpose for this walk, that she wanted people to know she honored the goddess. Farmers would also see the four soldiers from the palace and know that the king had returned his allegiance to Eurynome. These were valuable messages to give.

But not the message I seek. She needed to hear from the Mother herself that Brizo would succeed, but she did not know if Eurynome would speak to her. Her heart pounded, and she did not know how she would get through the next few days of waiting if the goddess did not come.

And I'm tired. She looked up at the tree-covered mountains that now towered above her. Seen from the shrine, they resembled the mountains that sheltered her home city, and she had thought she and her companions would come to the canyon that birthed the river well before the sun rose to its zenith. When the mountains began to loom over her long before her party reached their base, she understood that these were much taller and much steeper. The soldiers told her it would be another half a handspan before they arrived.

At least the valley was flat. Walking beside the quiet flowing river was not hard work. Just long. Her mind looped back to worry, but she shook her head to chase those thoughts away.

Enough walking in silence! Thalassai needed some distraction from the questions that plagued her. She realized that she did not really know Selene's story even though her tale had been told at the celebration feast. That night, Thalassai had been so dazed by the events of the day, so relieved to see her brother again, she had only really half listened to Melanion's adventure. It was time to reach out.

"I would like to hear how my brother came to the shrine you served, and about your journey with Dermios to this valley."

"Your brother's journey with Panacea was the darker one." Selene spoke of leading Melanion and Panacea to the entrance of the tunnel beneath the mountain, then told of her own journey with Dermios taking the horses through the high passes.

As she listened, Thalassai realized that this young woman had made a huge sacrifice. She stood up for Melanion against the will of the high priestess at the shrine on the far side of the Boundary Mountains. That disagreement had cost her, and Selene could not return to her home. That must pain her even though Asira welcomed her into the goddess' community in this valley.

Listening to Selene speak of the visit of Hades, God of the Dead, Thalassai shivered despite the heat. "I cannot imagine facing him. You must have been terrified."

"He is fearsome," said Selene, "but Eurynome came that night as well."

"You also have spoken to the goddess?" asked Metia, their young guide. Awe made the girl's voice little more than a whisper. "I thought only the priestess could claim this. But both of you…"

"Eurynome came to our fire to meet the God of the Underworld and to buy his assistance," said Selene.

Will she come today? Thalassai did not know if there was enough need in her pilgrimage. If their guide was right that these visits were unusual, she could not count on the goddess coming in person. *But I need help to know if I have done right!*

Thalassai's thoughts became a maze of all the choices she could have made, the different paths she could have taken. She needed a lighter conversation. She turned to Metia. "How long have you lived at the shrine?"

"I have been there since the winter solstice. My family asked if I could be schooled at the shrine for a year, and the priestess welcomed me. It is a sacrifice for them. I am the oldest, and they will have to hire help from neighbors for planting and harvest." Pride took over the girl's voice. "Not all the outlying families will ask for education for their girls, but Pa and Ma were determined." Metia held up the basket. "The priestess sends gifts like this to help. She is pleased they chose to educate a daughter."

A year at the shrine, thought Thalassai, *for a girl who will farm at the edge of the valley her whole life.* She could see it was a gift and a sacrifice. They were passing another farmer's plot, and this time Thalassai touched her forehead to acknowledge the family working there. They in turn bowed their heads to her party. *If these will be my people, I need to honor their efforts.* Perhaps as a member of the palace family, she could encourage more families to educate their daughters.

When they reached the place where the valley met the base of the mountains, Thalassai's eyes were drawn upward. The mountains filled half the sky. She saw five circling birds, a family of eagles riding the air currents high in the blue sky. Her heart lifted as she watched the soaring birds, even though the massive mountain felt like a weight upon her.

Metia pointed to a hut that sheltered under the wall of mountain with a large garden where a young boy worked. "My home is here. When I was younger," she said, "I hated the fact that in winter the sun's heat did not reach us until after the zenith. But in storms, I felt cradled by the arms of rock that reach into our valley."

The boy looked up from his planting. "Ma! She's here!" He ran up and wrapped Metia in a hug worthy of Herakles. A moment later, a woman came from behind the house to embrace her daughter.

"Ma, this is the princess from Tiryns who saved our

river," Metia stepped back so her mother could greet Thalassai. Her brother stood right against his mother's side staring at the princess with wide eyes.

"The river flows, and our vegetables flourish. Grain grows lush and seems in a hurry to make up for the weeks of drought." The woman put her hands together over her chest and bowed low. "We are so grateful to you and to Mother Eurynome."

Thalassai blushed. "I didn't do a lot. My brother helped. So did Selene here, and Prince Brizo."

"Tales travel to the outskirts here in pieces," Metia's mother said, "but we have heard that both princes of Ephyra played a role."

Thalassai pursed her lips together. Prince Aphoron's role had been to kidnap her. Though that had brought her to the valley, it was not a role she appreciated. Still, this was not the moment to raise that point. She forced a smile to her lips and kept her voice bright. "We go to thank the goddess herself at the river's birthplace. Perhaps another time Metia can return and tell the full tale."

From the sheltered farm, the soldiers of Ephyra led them into the shadow of the mountain and a deep canyon. The air grew colder, and Thalassai rubbed her arms with her hands. As the canyon narrowed, the water of the river bubbled and gurgled over smooth rocks, filling the air with bright sound. The path wound between gnarled oaks whose branches stretched for the light, which could only reach directly into this narrow, sheltered place at mid-day.

A rivulet fell from the rock beside the path. Thalassai put her hand in the water. Back in the valley, the water in the irrigation channels had been warm, but this felt cold as the deepest ocean. She leaned her head back and looked straight up at the sides of the canyon towering over them, leaving only a thin band of blue sky.

"Here we must enter the river, Princess," one of the soldiers said with a hushed voice. "It is a cold walk."

"It's the walk I came for." Thalassai accepted the supporting arm her bodyguard offered and stepped into the river. Ice-cold water flowed quickly over her calves, and her feet slipped on the rocks. She saw that Ephyran soldiers supported Metia and Selene, while the others led them deeper into the canyon.

Before long, her feet were numb, and she was more than thankful that she could lean on the soldier's arm. The water was colder than anything she had ever experienced. She had heard that on the tops of the mountains near Olympus, water turned solid and white in mid-winter, but she had never imagined feeling something that cold.

Her foot slipped. "Oh!" The exclamation escaped before she could stop herself, and the soldier helped her catch her balance.

"Are you all right?" Selene asked. "Do you want to rest?"

The river touched the canyon walls on both sides. There was no place to sit, no way to climb from the water unless they went back. She thought of her brother passing this way just five days earlier. If he could do it, so could she. "I am anxious to see the gate," she said.

"It's not much farther," said one of the Ephyran soldiers. "Soon you'll see the marvel of the Mother's gift."

Thalassai hoped he was right. Her feet could not feel the rocks of the riverbed, and with every step, she felt she might fall. The sun heated her hair even as her feet froze. It was a strange sensation.

"We arrive," said one of the other Ephyrans. "This is the bowl and the gate that births the river!"

As the walls of the canyon fell back to create a wide circle, Thalassai stopped. She felt tiny looking up at the three majestic mountains that rose straight up around this quiet pool of water. No wind reached this deep, sheltered place. Straight ahead, a dark cave stood above the pool, and a deep crack ran upward from the cave. The waters gently flowed around her, and Thalassai felt comforted. This was the place that gave life to the valley. She took a deep breath.

Are you here, Eurynome? Thalassai asked. She thought she heard a warm gentle voice answer, *Always.*

I have questions to ask you. Thalassai looked around for the goddess. There was no one in the water except those she came with. "Where are you?" she whispered.

"The Mother is here in the water, and in the trees that cling to the cliffs above us," said Selene. "She is the life of all."

But I want to see you. She needed to know if Brizo would be safe, and where her brother was. She needed to know if what she had chosen was right.

Again, she heard the whisper of a voice, *Open your ears.*

Thalassai's face tightened. This whisper was not what she came here to find. She wanted the goddess herself. Then, she realized she was pouting. If her long-time servant from Tiryns were here, she would remind Thalassai that a pout did not suit a princess. "Rage at wrong, object to trouble, but do not pout," was that servant's constant advice.

You know what you need to know, whispered the goddess in her ear.

But I don't know if Brizo will succeed, Thalassai objected. Then she realized that she did not really want the answer to her question ahead of time. He was beyond her reach and unable to withdraw from the task. She did not want to be told if he was doomed to failure; she would rather trust in his wisdom and hope for success.

Suddenly, Thalassai understood that what she wished for was a promise that he would conquer the monster, but not even the goddess could give that. It was the same with her brother: no one could know in advance how that hunt would play out.

Thalassai closed her eyes. She breathed the cool air of this sheltered bowl and smelled the sharpness of rock and mountain. She accepted the heat on her head, and the numbness of her feet. She sensed the movement of water beneath the surface. She knew that just as the veins of her body carried blood through her limbs, this river carried life to every part of the valley.

Turning to look back along the river and the canyon, Thalassai pictured herself following the flowing water back out to the farms, back to the shrine and on to the palace. The gift of the Mother would accompany her, strengthen her. It would be enough.

Thalassai saw Selene watching her. She smiled. "I think

we can go back now."

Selene also smiled. "I am glad to have stood in this place. Life rises here from the depths of darkness and the border of the underworld."

She saw the Ephyran soldiers nod. "We have offered our thanks to the Mother," one said. "We'll not wander from her ever again."

"Forever is a long time," said Selene.

Thalassai met her eyes. Why did Selene, servant of the Mother's shrine, open any possibility of a different path than following Eurynome?

Selene shrugged slightly. "The Mother has always taught us to attend to this moment, the path right in front of us."

"Then for today, we'll lean on her protection and return to our lives and our tasks." Thalassai leaned again on her guard's arm. "Let's go before my feet are too numb to walk at all!"

Chapter Nine

Tenth day after the full moon

With his hand on the tiller, Brizo watched the single white sail billow as he tacked across the light wind from the north. The second ship followed precisely the same path in the quiet waters. The dolphins that had followed all day shifted their track as well. Their presence gave Brizo a sense of ease: experience had taught that no predators were near as long as these swimmers followed.

Brizo steered the boat around a small island that rose as high as two ship-masts from the water. Swirling patterns had been cut by waves into the rock. There was a hint of green at the top of the cliff, but nothing grew on the sheer face. "Watch for outcroppings," he called to Apro, whom he had assigned to the prow as watcher.

The sailor did not even raise a hand to acknowledge the command. *Fair enough,* Brizo thought. Apro knew his job in unknown waters. Sheer as the cliffs of this island appeared, there could be rocks just under the waves. He leaned into the rudder to steer the ship farther from that possibility.

Since they had put up the sail a handspan earlier, his companions had been sharing stories of shark hunts as they lounged on the rowing benches. These beasts and the larger whales were uncommon but not unknown in these waters. The eldest of Brizo's companions had hunted shark successfully, and the men hung on his story as they let the wind carry the boat forward.

When the storytelling had begun, Apro complained that it was bad luck to speak of sea monsters while on the water. Others ignored him, but he kept grumbling. That was when

Brizo ordered him to relieve the watchman in the bow. Looking at the man's back, Brizo wondered if this sailor was going to keep being difficult. It would not help morale if he continued complaining. *And he seems determined to undermine my authority.*

The successful story the older sailor told encouraged the others, but given Eurynome's concern, Brizo did not think this was an ordinary shark they hunted. Brizo ran through the tales of sea monsters he had heard since childhood. In many, it seemed that the beasts attacked at this time of day when the sailors rested from rowing and let the sail do the work. That had happened to Jason, according to the poets. When he and his crew came near the island of the sirens, the bird-women's captivating song drove them to take down the sail and row toward the hazardous rocks. In that story, Herakles realized what was happening and told Orpheus to sing. The glorious music of the master musician was stronger than the call of the sirens. Jason and his crew rowed safely past and journeyed on to achieve their hunt.

Brizo's crew were ordinary men, not demi-gods and heroes, but he would give his companions a strong fighting chance. When they got near Corfu, they would shift back to oars. He trusted them more than the wind. Poseidon could stir up a storm in an instant. That god might have left the area, but if he was looking for revenge, the Earthshaker could make the breeze disappear or call up a violent wind just when they met the white shark.

Studying the eastern horizon, he saw a break in the mountains of the mainland. He knew that marked the place where a river flowed into a fertile delta. They were getting close to their destination. He turned the ship so they angled north-west. When they passed the next small island, he saw a dark shadow above the water, the island of Corfu.

"River valley to the east," called Apro from the prow. "Steer dead straight for Corfu."

Brizo pressed his lips together. The sailor stated the obvious as if his captain had not noticed. *And he likes to give orders.* At least the captain of the second boat was following his lead precisely. He would have to find a way to keep Apro in line.

The boat bounced as they headed into the open channel between the mainland and the large island of Corfu. When they were close enough to pick out the shape of the shoreline, Brizo decided it was time to shift back to rowing. "Sails down," he called. "Oars in locks."

"Sails would take us in more smoothly," Apro objected.

"Watchers, be alert for any sign of the creature." Brizo held Apro's eyes until the sailor turned back to his post, then made sure the other captain acknowledged his call.

"Should we prepare weapons?" one of the sailors asked.

"A spearman in front and one here beside the rudder," Brizo answered. Again, he relayed the instruction to the other boat. Rowers took up their positions.

"Brizo," said the man in the first bench, "the dolphins are gone."

"Alert!" Brizo shouted. There could be any number of reasons for the dolphins to leave, from boredom to hunger. But their departure might also indicate danger.

The boats pitched as they rowed directly into the wind. Only the caller now spoke as he set the timing for the rowers.

"Disturbance!" called the captain at the tiller of the second boat. "Straight behind!"

"Spears ready." Brizo scanned the water. A line of ripples ran across the surface as if a large school of fish in tight formation swam just under the waves. No fish swam at that speed.

The creature came.

A white fin cut through the surface, chasing the second boat. The creature would hit it in a moment.

"Hold!" Brizo commanded.

The men dug in their oars. The sailors stretched their necks to see what would happened to their companions' ship.

The fin disappeared as if the creature dove. Then, the boat keeled to one side, and several rowers were thrown from their benches. The captain at the rudder struggled to hold steady. The white fin surfaced beside the boat and carved a path back toward it. The boat twisted, and the captain was flung aside. A moment later, the fin appeared, driving straight toward Brizo.

The other captain steadied himself. "Three oars and the rudder gone," he called. "Bit right through."

"Oars up!" Brizo shouted. He let go of the rudder, and the ship turned slowly across the wind. The oarsmen could right it when the creature passed. The fin dove out of sight a ship-length behind them. *Where will you attack?*

Something hit the boat from below and it spun. A sharp crack right beneath him, and he knew the rudder was cut through. "Straighten us out, then oars up!" The rowers pulled the boat back into line.

"It comes again!" One of the sailors pointed to the fin that came straight at the side of the boat. "Can it bite through the hull?"

Just as the creature reached them, it twisted, pressing its body against the side of the ship. The boat listed, and men swayed on their benches.

The spearman beside him spoke up. "I can see its back. Do I throw?"

Brizo hesitated for one second. If they only angered the creature, it would do no good, but it felt wrong to sit like a toy for it to play with. "All your might."

The creature came up on the other side, tearing one oar then ramming the side of the ship. The boat tipped, taking on water. Two men started bailing. The spearman waited until the white fin rose on his side of the boat. He drew back his arm and threw.

The spear bounced off the shark's tough hide as it would off a bronze shield. The creature swung its head out of the water, showing teeth sharp as knives, then it dove. The water slowly calmed, and both ships stilled.

"Didn't even wound it," said the spearman.

"Row for shore," Brizo called. "Neither of us waits for the other. Get to land."

Suddenly, the fin appeared right beside the other boat, and the shark rammed the prow. With no rudder, the boat spun and rocked, but the rowers straightened it and pulled hard. A crack and another sailor was thrown from his bench, his oar broken.

Brizo picked up a spear. His hand clenched it hard. They were going to lose more of the oars, but without a rudder, he could not order the sail up.

"Straight ahead!" called Apro. "It's coming!"

"Row hard! We'll try to ram it," Brizo shouted. "Be ready to lift oars. Make the call, Apro."

Apro glared over his shoulder, then turned back to the water. "Row. Row hard. Steady. Lift!"

With one motion, the rowers lifted their oars. The creature's fin turned, skimming past on the port side of the boat. Its tail thrashed, and it turned away. At two ship-lengths out, it turned and rammed the boat.

The creature surfaced, jaws open wide. Brizo threw his spear into its mouth. The weapon bounced out, but the creature halted. A narrow stream of blood flowed from its mouth.

"Hard forward," Brizo called. His men responded with all their strength.

Again, the shark harried one ship and then the other. The rowers lifted their oars on command, and no more were lost, though the ships spun each time the shark hit. Ever so slowly, the shore approached. Four ship-lengths out, and the shark stopped hitting them. The white fin circled once, and again. Then, with a slash of its tail, it swam away.

Brizo watched the creature cut a straight line away from them toward the north, watched until he could not distinguish the fin from the whitecaps of the waves. He did not think they had injured it enough to drive it away. More likely, the beast knew it had forced them to land.

The sailors put their backs into rowing. They had seen their enemy, angered it. They had lost several oars and both rudders. They now knew it could cut through oak like a blade through unripened cheese.

"Where do we land?" called the captain of the other boat.

"First beach," called Brizo. They would not risk sailing to the nearest village in case the beast returned. This night they would set up camp, and in the morning, they would cross over land to find the nearest fishing village for supplies and information. The shark had won this first encounter.

Chapter Ten

Tenth day after the full moon

As they climbed the last rise to the palace, Thalassai's
legs felt heavy as stone. Her shoulders were stiff and her
whole body exhausted from the long, hot walk back from
the river's gate. At the entrance to the courtyard, she paused.
In a moment, she would cross into the palace to live as a
member of the royal family under the king's protection.

Thalassai looked up at the image of snakes carved into
the lintel. This ancient sculpture honored Eurynome. *I'm still
under the goddess' protection as well as the king's.* Even though
Eurynome had not come to her in person at the river's gate,
Thalassai had felt her presence. Walking back, she tried to
be aware of the goddess at work in the flowing river and the
growing fields.

Aware of her bodyguard waiting patiently with the
Ephyran soldiers, she realized that she still had her father
watching over her as well. In this new place where there
would be new customs and patterns, his influence would
help her. He never showed a sign of worry or uncertainty
even when he entered a new situation. She stood tall as he
would, lifted her shoulders, and smiled as she stepped into
the courtyard.

A teenage girl waited there. Thalassai recognized her
as Dorlas, the one who had looked after her during her
captivity. The girl bowed low. "Welcome, Princess. The head
servant, Mara, assigned me to guide you to your room."

"And where will my guard be housed? I expect him to
stay near me."

"Our captain will arrange for him," said one of the

soldiers.

Thalassai laid her palm above her heart. "Thank you for your escort today." Her bodyguard and the other soldiers bowed to her, then headed across the courtyard.

Thalassai turned back to the girl, relieved that she did not have to face the senior servant yet. Her status in the palace had changed since her captivity, but she was not confident she could convince Mara that she had authority. Mara had held the main responsibility for household details for a long time.

Thalassai glanced at the serving girl. It felt good to see someone familiar. She recalled the girl's shy and gentle nature. "When we get to my room, please bring me water to wash. I am hot and weary from my walk."

"Yes, Princess. Water is prepared for you, and fruit."

Thalassai wished again for a servant from home, one who would have readied the bathing chamber for her and provided her favorite food to revive her. Well, if this was going to be home, she could perhaps begin to influence things. "I would like olives as well. Then, I will rest from this exertion. I will take sweet bread when I awaken."

"I will try, Princess. But the king expects you at dinner. An emissary came today from the island of Paxos. The king invited some of the city nobles to a reception in his honor. Mara is readying clothes for you."

Thalassai sighed. The king had plans for her already, when all she wanted to do was rest. She understood the duty to honor visiting dignitaries, but she needed to establish some authority or the senior servant would continue to order her about. "I am sure Mara can look after the clothes. After I awaken from my nap—which I simply must take even if it is short—I will have you do my hair. You did a complicated braid when I first came that would look well this evening."

"Thank you, Princess." Dorlas hesitated. "You will speak to Mara?"

Thalassai pursed her lips together. Clearly, Dorlas was afraid of the older woman. Thalassai would have to stand up for herself.

***

The sun was setting when Dorlas wakened Thalassai from her rest. "Princess, there's not much time to get ready."

Thalassai sat up on the sleeping rug. "I feel refreshed, and will look much better for having slept. I will splash the sleep from my eyes, freshen my face. Then, you can do my hair."

"Mara found you a beautiful robe for tonight. She's been going through the clothes of Prince Brizo's mother for you, and aired them in the sunshine this afternoon. They had been stored since her death five years ago. The queen's robes have been stored even longer."

Thalassai expected that Brizo's mother, the king's concubine, had dressed well, but it might be nice to go through the queen's clothes when she felt more confident of her status.

Dorlas bit her lip as if unsure about her next question. "The shrine has sent a necklace for you. Will you wear it tonight?"

Did Asira send it to show the king who holds power in this valley? Thalassai did not think the priestess played power games, so the action likely intended a simpler message, one she could agree to. "I will wear it to remind us all that it was Eurynome who restored the river and rescued the valley from drought."

Dorlas gently combed Thalassai's hair, smoothing the long chestnut tresses before beginning a complicated braid that started at the top of her head. The girl's touch relaxed her. She closed her eyes and let the servant care for her. *It's good to know I can do this myself,* she thought, *but it's so nice I don't have to.*

"I picked some thyme from the garden to weave into the braid," Dorlas said as she worked. "The blue flowers are tiny, but will match the embroidery on the gown, and the scent is beautiful."

Thalassai usually chose a showier flower, but she did not want to offend the first person in the palace who had been kind to her. "That will be lovely."

Mara burst into the room. "Hurry up with that hair. The

king will be ready shortly, and the emissary and other guests are waiting outside the hall."

Thalassai sat straighter. "I have been taught to keep people waiting a little. Reminds them who wields power." Dorlas touched her shoulder to say she was done the braid. Thalassai stood. "I do not expect a bow every time my servants enter the room, Mara, but unless I have sent for someone, I do expect them to ask if I am ready for them." Only now did Thalassai turn to examine what Mara had brought. She held a beautiful green robe with spirals embroidered on the fold and at the base. The color would highlight the amber color of her skin and eyes. "That is a lovely choice for this evening."

"And it is time for you to be dressed." Mara hurried forward, but Thalassai raised a hand to stop her.

"You may give the robe to Dorlas, along with the clasps for the shoulders. She will help me." Thalassai knew she should not push too hard, but Mara's presumption annoyed her. "When I am dressed, you may place the necklace from the shrine on my neck."

"I have chosen ornaments from the concubine's wardrobe for you," said Mara.

Thalassai hesitated. Mara was right that she should present herself as royal, but she did not like feeling so dependent. Still, there was only so much she could say no to. "I will wear armbands and rings you have chosen, but I will wear the necklace the shrine provided, to proclaim the power of the goddess to those the king hosts this night. She is our protector, and the emissary from the isle of Paxos should see that we acknowledge her blessing."

Mara pursed her lips together, but handed the robe to Dorlas. Thalassai saw that the younger servant trembled slightly. She needed to be careful that Mara did not take revenge on other servants if Thalassai challenged her presumption of authority.

"Dorlas will have me dressed in a moment. You may send word to the king that I will attend him shortly." Thalassai watched Mara's face, until the woman bowed her head just a touch and left the room. *There. I did not quite dismiss her, but she will be coming back with my permission.*

Cold crept up Thalassai's back, and she shivered. There was so much to pay attention to in this new situation. And this evening, there would be a whole room full of people she did not know.

"You will warm up when you are dressed, Princess. Would you like a shawl?" Dorlas asked.

Thalassai sighed. It was best that others think it was the temperature that bothered her. "Ephyra is cooler in this season than my home, so a shawl might be well, at least in my rooms. Now help me into the robe, Dorlas. We need to meet my promise to be ready."

***

Thalassai sipped from the cup a servant handed her. The red wine was rich, as good as the best her father served. Unwatered as it was, it spread warmth through her body and relaxed her. This cup she would enjoy, but she would ask the servant to water the next.

Standing just off the dais to the king's right, she had a good view of the room where the powerful and the wealthy of the city mingled, and servants offered platters of food. She did not recognize anyone, but that was not surprising. At the celebration feast, she had been so focused on her brother that the rest of the evening remained a blur in her memory. This night she felt lonely. She wondered who among the younger women might become a friend. She cut off a sigh and put a smile back on her face. She returned her attention to the emissary from Paxos who stood in front of the king.

Thalassai listened as he described the damage to their ships caused by massive waves from the earthshakings of this winter and spring. After the first few, they had moved their ships farther up the beach and avoided more destruction, but the damage to their trading and fishing fleets had been significant.

The emissary had been to the shrine to offer thanks to the goddess for ending the earthshakings, and he spoke of needing specific goods, but as Thalassai listened to his droning voice coming back again and again to the damage, she thought he was angling for assistance replacing and repairing ships.

A young woman approached and bowed to her. "Princess Thalassai, we met at the feast the night your brother came."

Thalassai nodded. "I am afraid I do not remember your name. That evening was rather overwhelming."

"Of course. I'm Preema. I had the advantage—along with the rest of the city, I had known for two days who you were."

Thalassai blushed and looked down at her cup. She remembered how it had felt, as a captive, to walk through the city the day she arrived with all eyes on her.

"When Prince Aphoron escorted you to the palace," Preema continued, "you held yourself so straight and so tall." The young woman paused. "News of your beauty and your strength spread through the city. We all started to believe that you could save us." She met Thalassai's eyes. "In the end, it worked out differently than we expected, but your strength inspired us to hope."

I did not feel strong, Thalassai thought, but it was good to know she was able to hide her fear, at least from people who did not know her. "Thank you for coming to speak to me," Thalassai said. "It is strange not to know anyone. Tell me about yourself. Are your parents merchants here?"

"My family has an orchard quite near the city, and we raise sheep among the apple trees. We also own a ship, and recently we became patrons of a weaver."

"Your family is busy," said Thalassai.

"I have three brothers," said Preema. "My father believes that he must provide a business for each of them. So far, sailing is all any of them cares about. One is to be married this summer, and I think our father will insist he stay in the valley then."

"And you?"

"You mean, when will I be married?"

"If that is what you want, but I wondered which of the family businesses interests you."

"If you promise not to tell my father, or my mother."

Preema leaned closer and lowered her voice. "I am interested in improving the wool we produce. The weaver's work is fine, but it can only be as good as the fibers provided." Preema smiled shyly. "My parents don't let me spend much time with the sheep, but that may shift when my brother is married. I am friendly with his wife-to-be, so I hope to spend more time at the farm."

"A good dream. I hope it comes to pass for you. Are your brothers in the city now?"

Preema looked down. "Two are. One is with the Prince Brizo on the mission to Corfu. They should have arrived at the island before dark today. I hope they conquer the beast quickly." She looked up and met Thalassai's eyes. "I worry about my brother."

Thalassai's smile faded. "Prince Brizo, my brother, your brother, all travel into danger while we women wait in the city wondering."

"There was a woman traveling with your brother. Would you rather be on the road with him?" asked Preema.

Thalassai swirled her cup. To be honest, she was glad she was not racing after Aphoron or sailing into the dangerous waters where the white shark lurked. "I suppose not."

She pushed the worry aside. She did not want it to show in her face, draw questions from these strangers. "I have stood still long enough. Would you walk with me through the room? You could remind me of names I should know, introduce me to any I simply must meet."

"Certainly, Princess."

"Please call me Thalassai." Surely, this young woman had sufficient status that it was acceptable to invite her to use her name. "Just walk slowly. I need time to repeat the names in my head so I don't forget this time."

"Of course, Prin....Thalassai," said Preema. "You can always ask me again if you need to."

"My memory is quite good when I am not overwhelmed." Thalassai realized how relaxed she felt. It helped so much to have someone to accompany her in the crowded room.

Chapter Eleven

Eleventh day after the full moon

Brizo stepped from the trees. A steep rocky hill led down to a narrow pebbled beach. A few hardy shrubs clung to crevices but with no fresh water in sight, only tough yellow shore grass grew along the shore. Apro and the other sailor stepped up beside him.

"Again a cove with no one in it," said Apro.

"Streams are rare on this part of this island," said Brizo. "Spreads the villages out."

"How far are we going to have to walk, then?" Apro kicked a stone out of his way.

"Until we get to the first village," said Brizo.

"Better walking than facing that beast," said the other sailor.

Brizo scanned the empty ocean. He had not seen a fishing boat or a trading vessel all morning. Across these once friendly waters, he could see the outline of the mainland and its mountains, so close but completely cut off from Corfu as long as the creature patrolled this strait.

Brizo ignored Apro's muttering and led the way up the hill. At the top, the forest was thick, and the only paths they found appeared made by deer. In the past, people traveled from village to village by boat. Now people would have to cut paths to move around the island, at least until the shark had been dealt with.

Can we defeat the beast? Their first encounter gave him doubts. They could not make a second attempt until they had new rudders and oars. Brizo had left to the main body of sailors the task of felling wood to replace what the shark had broken.

He had sent three other companions across the island to the west to learn what they could about the shark. Perhaps someone had seen a weakness in the great white beast or knew more of the creature's pattern of attack.

The sun had crossed the zenith when they climbed a ridge and saw the mud huts of a village in the cove beneath them. Boats had been pulled up away from the shore. At intervals along the beach, poles planted in the sand secured fishing lines extending into the water. Women worked among the houses, and vegetables grew along both banks of a stream. As they climbed down, young children called out to announce the arrival of visitors. An old woman laid down her hoe and came to meet them.

"You are strangers to us, though you come across the land," she said.

"Our boats landed a morning's walk to the south," Brizo said.

"You met the beast that holds our people prisoner."

Brizo noted that the woman made this a statement, not a question. "It attacked us as soon as we approached your island."

"You are fortunate to have made land at all. No one has successfully crossed from the mainland since the red moon. Where are you from?"

"Ephyra. The goddess Eurynome informed us of your plight and set my city the task of aiding your people."

"Praise the goddess for trying," said the old woman, "but you are now marooned among us, or have condemned yourselves to death."

"Do not give up on us too quickly. We drew blood on our first encounter," said Brizo. "We could use more information about the creature before we try again."

"Drew blood and more anger." The woman frowned at the ground, and then looked up at Brizo with a sad expression on her face. "You are here on the island now and caught with us in this trouble. Our men are hunting. Much as they would rather fish, we need meat of some kind, and the longlines do not produce much. We begin to wonder if the schools of fish have been chased away from the coast."

"Our companions don't expect us back until tomorrow. We will wait for the men to return. Is there work we can assist with while we are among you?"

Apro muttered an objection under his breath, but the woman looked at Brizo with new appreciation. "Always."

***

"Others came from your city in the past." The headman of the village dipped bread in the bowl of stew he held on his lap. "I have not met you, though you say you are a son of the king."

"My older brother Aphoron led the company on other visits," said Brizo, "though I have been among the sailors."

"Where is your brother, then?"

Brizo hesitated. "He is on another mission." That was true enough. No need for these villagers to know that it was his own mission, not his father's.

"Unless Herakles comes, it will be the same. The beast chews through wood like barley straw."

"Can it open a hole in the boat itself?"

"It has not. I suppose there is no purchase for its jaws." The man shook his head sadly. "After the first attacks, we went to the center of the island to cut wood from the hardest of trees. We smoked it and oiled it, and still the creature cut through our oars as soon as we crossed into the deep water." The headman stirred the stew in the bowl with his bread. "We make food from land creatures and wear out our sandals walking. This is not the life we were born to." He shook his head then met Brizo's eyes. "But it is our life, and yours now. Your father is bereft of a son. You are one of us."

"You did not expect aid to come from the mainland at all," said Brizo, "yet here I am with two crews of determined sailors. Let us work together."

The headman put down his bowl. "We can speak again in the morning."

Frustrated as he was with the attitude of the headman, Brizo knew he had been dismissed for the night.

***

Eurynome stood on a sandy beach at the southern tip of Corfu. In the west, the stars of the snake touched the ocean waters. That constellation told the tale of the beginning when she had danced on the ocean waters and called up four huge snakes to become the great rivers that nourished the lands she watched over.

Tonight, the dark water looked peaceful, but somewhere beneath that quiet surface, a dangerous beast lurked. She reached her thoughts out into the ocean, but she could not locate the shark.

Eurynome longed for the waters of her own rivers, but the people of Corfu sought her blessing and her help. The second prince of Ephyra had responded to that need, and it was time for her to see how young Brizo was doing. In her mind, Eurynome called to the four-lined snakes common on this island. She woke one in each of the villages in the south of Corfu and asked them to find Brizo.

A restless itch climbed the base of her neck as if someone called to her. Eurynome stepped into the water, letting the gentle waves lap against her ankles. She reached again to feel the presence of the beast, to understand its hunger and its anger.

A sudden gust swept across the water, swirled in front of her. A waterspout climbed from the waves. The torso of a man rose, hair unkempt as seaweed.

"Oceanus," she said, greeting the ancient titan. Perhaps this was why she sensed someone calling. "It has been a very long time."

"We have not met since a time the lands have forgotten, but you did me a great favor, returning my daughter to me."

"Only the shade of your daughter," Eurynome said. The long-dead girl had risen from the underworld to describe to the king of Ephyra how fickle Poseidon could be. "The dolphin you sent carried her shade home?"

The titan nodded. "She rests at peace in the shadowland of our island. I have come to pay my debt."

"She did us a service, telling her story. There is no debt."

"There is." Oceanus' voice rumbled like a wave pounding rocks. "She acted by her choice. Helping her to return home was a gracious service to me. The information I provide is payment."

Eurynome nodded. The gods and even the titans could not freely interfere in the work of another immortal. Paying a debt, however, would be understood. "I will accept what you tell me as full payment."

The titan spread his arms wide. "Years ago I created a sea creature to protect the shores of my island from the Greeks who raided there. The men of this land extend their fingers far beyond their proper reach. In my anger, I made the beast too hungry. She kept my fishing folk on the shore." The titan closed his fists. "I bound her in a cavern, and for a generation of men, she slept. Just before the red moon you called into the sky, Poseidon located the cavern, carried her to these waters, and woke her."

"Such a style this Olympian god chooses. Seek new followers by bringing an unexpected threat." Eurynome shook her head. "I suppose he will promise to protect the people from it."

"He will not succeed. She has drawn male sharks to her side. She carries young within her even now. When her brood is born, no ship will be safe on this coast or beyond."

Eurynome drew a sharp breath. The danger was worse than she had known. "This is news indeed. Your debt is well paid."

"After taking my only daughter, the Earthshaker stole what I created. I will be in your debt again if you thwart this scheme." Oceanus spun, drawing the waters into a swirling spiral. He dove into the whirlpool.

Eurynome waited for the waves to quieten, pondered what she had been told. The hunt had gained an urgency she had not anticipated. She rubbed the back of her neck, wondering if the restless feeling would now disappear. Then, she felt a tug. One of the snakes had found Brizo.

***

In the hut that the villagers had cleared for them, one of the sailors snored, but Brizo did not think Apro slept. As soon as they were alone there, Apro had begun a litany of complaints about the headman's refusal to help, about the isolation of villages on this island, about Aphoron's desertion. When he complained that Eurynome should have left Corfu to the shark, Brizo silenced him. Apro glared with hands clenched, but laid down with his face to the wall.

Restlessness made Brizo's hands and feet itch. He was not ready to sleep. He pushed back the door curtain and stepped out into the cool air of night. Stars covered the dark sky, and the constellation of Herakles appeared to stand on the hill to the west. He wondered if there was a shrine to Herakles in these hills, if he might go there to summon the hero to his aid.

Watching the twinkling stars, Brizo remembered the story of the hydra, the many-headed monster that Herakles had killed. The hero had not known how to accomplish that hunt when he began it, and at first the hydra seemed impossible to kill. It was during the fight itself that Herakles had the idea of using fire to keep the beast from growing new heads. Brizo relaxed his hands, his shoulders. Even Herakles had to feel his way forward, figure things out as he went. *One step at a time,* he told himself.

A movement at the base of one of the huts caught his eye. A four-lined snake slithered across the sand. Brizo moved toward it, and the snake froze as if it hoped to hide in the shadows. He grabbed it just behind the head, and lifted it gently. It was young, not quite the length of his arm.

Brizo ran a finger along the head of the snake. It gazed at him with eyes that seemed intelligent. He could not summon Herakles, but there might be a way to call the goddess. He moved across the beach toward the water. "Eurynome," he called softly. He stepped into the waves. He felt for the rhythm of the retreating tide. "Eurynome, Eurynome," he whispered in time with the waves.

"He is a beauty, is he not?" The mother goddess stood beside him and caressed the long body of the snake he held.

"He is hungry though. Let him hunt."

Brizo stepped toward the dry sand and released the creature. It raised its head and swayed for a moment in front of the goddess, then slithered back toward the huts.

"You have met the sea creature," Eurynome said.

"We lost both rudders and some oars in that encounter. We need to strengthen our wood to venture out against it, though we're told traditional ways to do that have failed. "

"I cannot provide equipment for you," Eurynome said.

Brizo heard the denial, but sensed more in the Mother's voice. "You provided the snake."

Eurynome smiled and ran her fingers across his forehead, pushing his hair back. "You always were smarter than your brother. What is stronger than the wood you used?"

"Metal. But salt water pits it." Brizo saw the corners of the goddess' mouth rise slightly. Something in what he suggested…A thought came. "This time it does not need to last beyond the hunt." He thought Eurynome's lips curved more. "Oars of metal would be too heavy to row with." He tilted his head, watching her and thinking. "Perhaps a thin plating, a kind of armor for oar and rudder, but I have never heard such a thing."

"Armor for a boat that must fight a monster. It is a good thought." Eurynome stepped into the waves, letting the water wash around her ankles. "She is an ancient creature that Poseidon released."

"Poseidon again!" Brizo looked out across the waters, wondered where that god wandered this night, where the beast swam. "Is there anyone on Corfu with the skill to make armored oars?"

"Ask the headman," said Eurynome. "Get him to gather bronze for you, and try yourselves. You have a decent smith among your sailors?"

"We have more wood-crafters." Brizo thought for a moment. "Timon's father works in bronze."

"Get him to start." Eurynome stepped deeper into the water, closed her eyes as if feeling for a presence in the gentle waves. "There are males around her. She will soon brood. That must not happen."

Brizo imagined a clutch of creatures like the one that had handicapped his ships. He clenched his hands. "So the impossible task has become urgent."

"You are not one to give up." Eurynome smiled softly. "I have seen the large, warm-blooded sea monsters rise from the waves and roll, but never the sharks. I've always wondered if some part of their underside was thinner."

"How do we get at the underside of the creature?" Brizo posed the question, but to empty air above the ocean waves. The goddess was gone. He shook his head. The plan to armor oar and rudder seemed impossibly farfetched, and he wondered if the islanders would really be prepared to provide the necessary metal. And how would he get the shark to turn his belly to their spears?

He corrected himself. *Her* belly. Her pregnant belly. Soon this beast would release many small sharks into the water, and no one would sail again. This hunt was more than urgent. He shook his head. The Mother approved of the idea to armor the oars and rudder. He would use her approval of this plan to convince the headman to provide the metal they needed.

Chapter Twelve

Eleventh day after the full moon

Thalassai lounged on a bench cushioned with sheepskins as servants brought jar after jar of heated water to fill the terracotta tub in the bathing room of the palace. When they were done, Mara tested the full tub with her hand. "The water is adequately warm. Will you bathe now, Princess?"

"I will." She planned to enjoy this luxury of palace life.

"I am prepared to anoint you with scented oil when you are done," said Mara.

Thalassai cringed at the thought of Mara's heavy-handed massage. "Dorlas can do what is needed. She has the tool to clean around my nails." Thalassai was determined to get rid of the grime that weeding had pushed into the skin of her hands. "I am sure there are important tasks that need your attention, Mara."

Frown lines creased the senior servant's forehead. "If you are certain, Princess, I will leave you in the girl's adequate care."

"Dorlas is quite skilled enough," said Thalassai. "Her work on my hair drew compliments last night." Thalassai thought Mara might argue further, but the older woman schooled her face to a smile, and even gave a slight bow as she left the room. Dorlas looked worried, but Thalassai smiled at her. "Now help me into the tub. I plan to enjoy this."

Thalassai relaxed into the warm water. Dorlas massaged her right hand and carefully cleaned all the grit from under and around her fingernails. Dorlas was gentle but tentative. Thalassai considered how to get the girl to relax. "Tell me about your home, your brothers and sisters."

Dorlas started to talk. She gained confidence as she described each of the brothers and her one sister, the oldest in the family. Thalassai quickly lost track of the names and who was married or had children, but she let Dorlas talk as she worked. Thalassai leaned back in the water. This was wonderful. Soon, she would wash her hair, and then, when she was thoroughly clean, she would have Dorlas, with her gentle touch, rub scented oil into her skin. After half a moon of adventures, it felt good to be pampered.

***

Wearing a short linen robe and breathing in the rich scent of the oil that Dorlas had rubbed into her skin, Thalassai closed her eyes and enjoyed the feel of the girl's hands combing out the tangles in her hair. The door to her room swung open, and Mara charged in.

"The steward needs to speak to you. Now."

"I am hardly presentable," said Thalassai, though she was grateful the man had sent Mara to prepare for his entry. The previous steward, conscious of his great power, had barged straight in. "I will attend upon him as soon as Dorlas is done."

"No." Mara stepped forward, and this time bowed. "Princess, there is a problem. He would not discuss it with me, but he is extremely agitated."

Thalassai bit her lip. Whatever was going on, she could not ignore it. "Bring that shawl, please Dorlas." Thalassai stood, arranged her hair on her shoulders. "Show him in."

The steward had been waiting just outside the door. "You must come and act in place of the king to finalize an arrangement with the emissary. He waits in the throne room."

"You want me to give ceremonial approval for the agreement he and the king made?" Thalassai almost laughed. Then, she saw in the steward's face that he was completely serious.

"The emissary is upset. He planned to leave before the sun reached the zenith and has paced the throne room for a handspan already. He represents an important ally and must not be further angered."

"This is the king's agreement, not mine."

"But we cannot wake him. The doctor has been summoned. You must come."

Thalassai's knees buckled, and she sat. The king was ill!

The steward reached out his hands, pleading. "The king's servants allowed him to sleep late, but finally called me. I could not rouse him. Someone needs to deal with the representative from Paxos."

Now, she understood the steward's distress. The emissary would be anxious to depart. Even in well-known waters, the timing of a sea voyage was chosen carefully. She trembled with frustration. She had been relaxing for the first time in half a moon, and now she had to deal with this.

Mara returned with a light woolen robe dyed a bright yellow. For once, the unruffled competence of the senior servant was a relief. "Dorlas, a simple braid, please." She felt the girl hesitate. "You can begin now." The girl stepped forward and smoothed her hair. Her fingers worked quickly.

Thalassai thought of her father and how many of these meetings she had attended with him. She could do this. "If you would wait outside the room, Steward, I will dress in a way that honors the emissary."

"But be quick, Princess," he said.

Thalassai frowned. Irritation at the command sparked a thought. "And send for Asira."

"Pardon?" The steward frowned.

"Asira, the priestess of the goddess." Thalassai turned her head slowly, so that she did not disturb Dorlas' work. She met the steward's eyes. "Send for her at my command. If the king is ill, she will be of service to him." She waited but the steward did not move. "By the time you have found a servant to send for the priestess, I will be ready." She made a motion with her hand that she had seen her father give many times, and finally the steward bowed and left the room.

"You may suffice after all," Mara said. "Give me the day

robe, and we'll arrange this one. You do remember our relationship with Paxos is complex. We trade…"

"Mara, please. Give me space to think." While Mara arranged the fold of the robe and used silver spirals to pin the shoulders, Thalassai's thoughts raced. She wanted to think about the king's illness, but she pushed that question aside. She ran through what she remembered of the negotiations the night before. She had not paid attention to the final arrangements, but who could have imagined she would be formalizing the agreement?

Thalassai stopped her wishing. The steward could handle the details. Her part was to acknowledge the honor Ephyra gained through this cooperation. She played over the language of brothers, the way her father liked to refer to their neighbors. If that reference was unusual here, she could smile and speak of the gifts she brought from the distant south.

"You are ready." Mara said.

I don't feel ready. But it is time. "Open the door, Mara." Thalassai waited for the steward to enter. "Remind me of the details of the agreement as you lead me to the hall." *I am new here and hardly know my way around the corridors, let alone the politics*, she thought. As she listened to the specifics that had been negotiated, she wondered again what kind of illness had struck the king. She would go to him as soon as she finished with the emissary.

***

"I expected King Kratos to see me off," said the emissary, "though I am pleased to admire your beauty again."

The steward flinched, but Thalassai managed a quiet smile and a slight nod of acknowledgement. "The king is meeting with the priestess of Eurynome." *Though it is true Asira is going to him, my words hide more than they tell. I may be good at this yet.* "Our valley and your island have escaped from the earthshakings, and we need to acknowledge the goddess' assistance."

"My chief sent offerings to the shrine, though it is hard to understand why the goddess took so long to stop the damage. Our people were hard pressed as wave after wave crashed against the shore. But enough of that. We trust the mountain will shake no more."

Thalassai frowned slightly. She did not like the implied criticism. Surely this man would not consider seeking aid from someone other than the Mother. "Several paths met on the beach the day the goddess intervened. All those strands had to come together. We mere humans cannot hurry or force such things."

"It is usually the old like me who preach patience." The emissary smiled. "Beauty and virtue both you bring to Ephyra. The king and princes are indeed fortunate."

Enough of these compliments, Thalassai thought. "I will have to wait for another time to enjoy more of your flattery." She was pleased the emissary reddened a little. "The king is content to provide seasoned wood from our store for your urgent need. We know how long it would take to prepare green lumber for a good ship. I believe it has been loaded, Steward?"

The steward looked relieved that the interview was coming to an end. "Yes, Princess."

"Then, please send an escort to take our guest to his ship. He is eager to return home, I am certain."

The emissary bowed. "Perhaps I will be privileged to return and deliver my people's thanks to you in person."

"The king will be pleased to receive you as often as you are sent." Thalassai nodded to acknowledge his bow and turned with all the dignity she could muster. She wanted to get away from this man whose words were smooth as olive oil, but she walked slowly back to the door through which she had entered. Dorlas waited in the corridor.

"Asira arrived and has gone to the king. Do you want me to take you to them?" the young woman asked.

Thalassai leaned back against the wall. "A moment, please." She needed to take a couple of breaths by herself before she headed to the next encounter. As she assessed the meeting with the emissary, she thought she had held her own, not given anything away. The king would be satisfied when he got the steward's report. *When will that be?* She closed her eyes, but she heard Dorlas shuffling her feet. The girl was right. She could not just stand in the corridor. She needed to keep going, to face whatever would happen next.

Thalassai thought of Brizo and his companions facing the white monster in the waters of Corfu. There was no way to inform him of his father's illness, and he could not leave the hunt he had undertaken. Still, she wished he were back already. *Goddess watch over him. Give me strength and some of the patience I pretended to have!*

Chapter Thirteen

Eleventh day after the full moon

"Mel!" Panacea inched her mare up beside Melanion. "A breather. For the horses."

"I could use a stretch, too," called Dermios.

Melanion pressed his lips together. He longed for an open road where the horses could eat up the distance with a swift gallop. As it was, it would be after the sun crossed the zenith the next day before they reached the land-bridge that Corinth controlled.

"First stream we cross," Melanion said. He knew Panacea was right. They had risen before dawn and begun their journey by the light of the moon. Though small as a slice of olive, its light had enabled an early start. Now, a short rest and water would strengthen the horses.

Before long, they came to a narrow stream. "Slow boy. We'll take a break." Melanion placed a hand on the trotting stallion's neck. The horse eased his pace to a walk, but blew from his nostrils as if he too objected to the need for rest.

When she dismounted, Panacea rummaged in her bags for the restorative herbs she regularly fed the horses. She gently rubbed their noses as they took the leaves.

Dermios drank from a leather flask, then handed it to Panacea. "You need some of your own medicine. Can't believe how much I've come to appreciate the awful stuff you brew."

Panacea took the flask with a shake of her head. "I am glad we will soon arrive at my home shrine," she said. "I need to replenish my stores. I can't believe how much I have used to keep you going."

"Your gifts have been of great service to us, Panacea," said Melanion, "but we understand you may be needed at the shrine. We have kept you from your usual tasks for almost half a moon."

"No point making plans until we have a sense of what Aphoron is up to," she said. "We'll learn something at the land bridge. He cannot avoid the Corinthian guards there, and so when we get there, we will hear something about where he is going."

"This is true." Melanion touched her hand as she passed him the flask. "But I hate chasing him, letting him set the path."

The black stallion lifted his head from the water and stomped the earth with his hoof. The chestnut shook his head, and the mare whinnied. The horses looked refreshed, did not show that they had been racing across the land for three days after a similar journey north.

"You're right, my friends. Time to go." Melanion's smile was tight and worried when he turned to Dermios and Panacea. "We continue the hunt."

Chapter Fourteen

Twelfth day after the full moon

Red light tipped the waves of the Gulf of Corinth in anticipation of the rising of the sun. *The color of fire,* Eurynome thought, *or the blood that comes with birth.*

The goddess shook her head. She knew that the sun was not reborn each day, that it shone on distant lands when it was night in Greece. Equating dawn with birth was too much like the Olympians' way of thinking. Those gods and goddesses actually taught their followers that when the sun set on Greece, the titan Helios made a dark journey through the waters under the earth to bring the sun back to rise the next day.

Eurynome closed her eyes as the first warm rays of this day caressed her face. She let the waters lap at her feet. Then, she looked out at the island where Poseidon's son the cyclops lived. Three days earlier, Aphoron had sailed to this island and continued east. Later this morning, he would land his ships near Corinth, and Melanion would reach the land bridge a few handspans later. She feared that Poseidon sent Aphoron to set off a rockslide of trouble.

Again, she shook her head. The south she could not reach, and she thought Melanion had the wisdom and strength to deal with whatever the Earthshaker planned there. Her sphere was north and west, and she had come this far south to enlist the aid of one who could help with Brizo's hunt. She followed a small stream inland to the clearing where Hephaestus had settled for this season. There, the God of the Forge worked at the fire, building the coals to provide the heat he needed for his metalwork.

Talia looked up from the pot she stirred on the smaller cooking fire. "I am getting used to preparing food for more than two," she said.

Hephaestus scowled. "This was a properly isolated valley until three days ago."

"I won't eat, thank you Talia. I came with a question."

Hephaestus stood as tall as his crippled leg allowed. "The question will imply a favor that you seek."

"That you can decide for yourself," said Eurynome. "I wonder if it would be possible to plate oars with a metal light enough to still allow the sailors to row."

"Highly unusual," said Hephaestus. "What advantage would there be in such an endeavor? Some new battle strategy?"

"You know I am not interested in warfare."

Hephaestus studied her face. "The bronze we use for a sword could not be made thin enough for the oar to be managed. A layer of tin would be light, but would it have the toughness you require? You will have to tell my why you seek this."

"The armor needs to turn back the teeth of an unnaturally large shark."

"A beast set loose by one of my relations? You know I cannot intervene in their plans."

Eurynome warmed her hands over the bright coals of his fire. "Poseidon has freed a monster that is terrorizing the island of Corfu."

"Poseidon again!" Hephaestus scowled into his fire. "I had a plan laid out for this day's work."

Talia held out a bowl of olives to Eurynome. "Even if you do not want to interfere, Hephaestus, we can be hospitable."

Eurynome took one of the plump black fruits. "These are lovely. They come from…" She pondered the taste carefully. "These were grown on Mount Pelion."

Talia smiled. "They came as payment from the prince of the city at the base of the mountain."

"They came by ship, I am sure." Eurynome turned back to meet Hephaestus' frowning stare. "I believe the God of Storm hopes that the only ones traveling by boat will be those who pay tolls to him. Trouble is that the shark will brood before the moon is full. Our waters will teem with beasts that can chew through oar and rudder. I do not believe Poseidon can control her children."

"Impossible," Hephaestus said.

"She speaks the truth, my love. I see it in her eyes."

"I mean that this cannot be allowed," said Hephaestus. "You think I can find a way to coat all the ships of Greece with metal her children cannot penetrate?"

"Just two ships, I hope. If those who hunt her succeed before she broods, our waters will be safe until your fellow Olympian comes up with another plan."

A growl rumbled from Hephaestus' wide chest. "Who have you thrown to the shark? Someone you don't like very much, I presume."

"Actually, the one who took the task is a favorite of mine. He and his companions are camped in a cove on the south of the island. I suggested he get the islanders to collect metal and see what his sailors could accomplish."

"Unless he's one I trained, he'll not accomplish much." Hephaestus pushed apart the coals of the fire so they began to cool. "A blend of tin with a little copper, and if I add...." He muttered too softly to himself for the goddess to hear.

Eurynome smiled. "I do not need to know the recipe."

"It will take time to discover an alloy that will last."

"She will birth her young before the moon is full," said Eurynome. "You and the hunters need to beat that deadline. Speed, not endurance, in this case."

"Perhaps. Until the Earthshaker has another idea. He is much too busy at the moment." Hephaestus lifted his crutch from where it leaned.

Eurynome reached out a hand to touch Hephaestus, but the god pulled away. "I could heal your hip," she said.

"Maybe. Maybe not. When I lean on my cane, it does not trouble me. I do not need to be in your debt."

"But I am in yours."

"I am doing this for myself, not you. For people to come for the tools I make, I need the waters of Greece free of this menace."

"As you wish. I will remember what I owe in my own opinion. Talia, Corfu is rugged but there are many old trees."

Talia smiled at Hephaestus, who shook his head and did not look up. "I will go along to make sure he does not take too much living wood for his hungry fires. I expect we will meet again."

Eurynome bowed to the nymph and turned away. A pain spread across the top of her head and down her neck. She rubbed her temples. Someone was calling her, but who was it this time? She needed to clear her thoughts. She bowed to Hephaestus and Talia and walked back the way she had come.

At the gulf, Eurynome let the waves touch her feet. She felt a hint of laughter in the lapping waters, Poseidon's pleasure in the progress of his ambitions. She closed her eyes and heard the flapping of wings. Looking south, she saw an owl flying across the water. She whispered a call, and it came and perched on her hand. She stroked its feathers.

"You have made a long journey, little one." The owl blinked and ruffled the feathers of its shoulders. "Do not bristle at me. I admire your strength. You are returning to Asclepius." Eurynome tilted her head, listening. "Perhaps a visit to the God of Healing is in order. I will see you there."

The owl opened its wings and lifted itself straight into the air. It looked down at the goddess from where it hovered. Then, she was no longer at the water's edge, and the owl made its own slower way north.

Chapter Fifteen

Twelfth day after the full moon

Morning sun streamed through the east windows of the empty throne room. The picture of the goddess in the water of the river's birthplace comforted Thalassai as she paced toward the door that led to the king's chambers. Surely Eurynome was watching over Ephyra and would see the need of her king. She stopped at the door, traced the four spirals carved into the wood. Beyond this door, along a corridor and inside his room, she knew the king lay on the sleeping rug unresponsive, trapped by a strange illness or some god's magic.

The previous day, nothing had roused him. The smallness of his frame lying still on the sleeping rug and the empty expression on his face had disturbed her, but for most of the day, Thalassai had remained there to watch over him. Asira went back to the shrine once, returning with herbs to treat him. He had not responded, and the priestess looked worried. The palace doctor tried two treatments with no more success. His whispered consultation with Asira had deepened Thalassai's concern. Neither knew the cause or an effective method to waken him.

Twice that day, the steward had requested her presence in the throne room. She appreciated his more deferential manner as he asked her to deal with concerns that could not be put off. It had been difficult given how little she knew of the economy of Ephyra, but with the steward's support, she found a way to sort through the issues.

Thalassai stifled a yawn. She had not slept well the night before. In truth, she had not wanted to sleep in case she succumbed to the spell that held the king. She had paced beside her sleeping rug until her legs would no longer hold her up. Even when she lay down, she kept her eyes open. Eventually, exhaustion won, and she slept. Relief filled her when she opened her eyes to the light of morning. She had seen the same relief in Dorlas' face.

As soon as she was up, Mara had attended upon her, reported that Asira had spent the night with the king and requested her presence. Thalassai ate slowly, fruit and then sweet bread. She delayed attending to the king as long as she could. Finally, she forced herself to rise and leave her room. She had gotten as far as the throne room before her courage slipped away.

I cannot stand at this door forever. Thalassai traced the four spirals once more and sent a prayer to the goddess, asking her to heal the king. She opened the door and walked toward the two soldiers who guarded the entrance to the king's chamber. One opened the door for her, and she stepped in. The air smelled of pine and lavender. She relaxed her clenched hands. She realized that she had expected the stench of decay or the putrid odor of sickness. Asira sat beside the sleeping rug, and the king's personal servant knelt beside her. The king lay still, his chest hardly moving as he breathed.

"Will you sit with him a while?" asked Asira.

"Of course," Thalassai said. Much as she would rather be anywhere else, it was the right thing to do.

Asira laid a hand on the king's forehead and called to him softly. There was no response, not even a flickering of his closed eyelids. "I will send Della with herbs in oil, but I am not certain what else to try." The priestess stood. "I must consult the priestesses of the other shrines. Perhaps one of them has seen a disease like this."

Thalassai cringed. She remembered looking up at the massive mountains, and Selene's story of the passes that crossed them. It would take time to send messengers to shrines on the other side of the mountains. "How long will it be before you hear back from the others?"

"This evening."

Thalassai frowned. "How can that be?"

"Thanks to the power of the goddess, we have a way to link minds," said Asira. "Always one of the people of the shrine watches in the sanctuaries so that we can call one another. If they do not know a cure, we will ask the Mother."

When Asira had gone, the room grew completely still. The servant said nothing. Thalassai shifted her position one way and then another. Her restlessness was not enough to break the silence, which began to feel like a stifling blanket.

I could sing. The only song that came to mind was the lullaby that her long-dead mother used to sing. The king did not need help to sleep, but somehow the words of every other song had flown from her mind.

The silence grew heavier, and Thalassai needed to break it. Perhaps she could sing the lullaby, since her mother had sung it as a promise that the dark would not last, that morning would come. Night had frightened her as a young girl. Darkness still had that power over her.

And this silence made her heart race and her chest tighten. She would break it. Thalassai drew in a deep breath. "I am going to sing," she said to the servant.

The man nodded once, unable to break the spell of silence himself. Thalassai sang two lines: "*Sleep is a seed, little one, the life of tomorrow hides in her.*" She swallowed. Her voice seemed so small. The servant nodded again, encouraging her.

Thalassai hesitated. The rest of the first verse was about deep sleep, remembering the story of Persephone and her season trapped in Hades' kingdom. That verse felt too dark to help.

My brother crossed by the edge of Hades' kingdom. And even the story of Persephone was about return: the goddess came back every spring. But the second verse of the lullaby was about waking so Thalassai decided to sing that.

"*Sleep is a seed, little one, she hides the yellow fruit of morning, prepares the juice for your waking. Choose a red grape for this night, a green one for the promise of dawn.*" The servant smiled at her, and her voice felt stronger. Another song came to mind, a song sung at the spring feast, but first she would finish this one. She started again and sang the lullaby through twice, holding to the promise that morning and awakening always came.

***

The steward visited twice that morning to check on the king. No supplicants had come so far this day, so Thalassai remained in the king's chamber. When the air became stuffy, she asked the servant to stir the basin of pine and lavender. The sweet, fresh scent revived her.

From time to time, Thalassai got up and walked circles in the room to release the cramps in her legs. The steward returned at mid-day, and a servant brought them fresh bread, cheese and olives. Someone had realized Thalassai's love for this fruit, likely Dorlas, and she appreciated that attention to her comfort. A short time later, Della arrived from the shrine with two small jars.

"Has the priestess determined the cause of the king's illness?" the steward asked.

"First, we designed a way to provide him what he needs to survive it." Della turned to the servant. "Please bring me a bowl of warm water and some honey." She knelt by the king and removed the stopper from one of the jars. A sharp scent rose from the oil inside. "This is a stimulant. We are not sure that the powder of coriander and hot pepper we mixed into the oil will rouse him, but it should keep him from descending into a deeper sleep. If he descends too deeply, there is little hope of waking him." Della pulled back the cover and anointed the king's arm with the oil.

"And the other jar?" Thalassai asked.

"Come, and kneel by his other arm." Della handed Thalassai the jar. "His body needs the essential salts we added to this oil."

Thalassai removed the stopper and sniffed the brownish liquid. Complex scents mixed with the olive oil, but she could not place the ingredients.

"Dip your finger as I do," Della instructed her, "and spread it lightly along his arm. His skin can absorb much of

102

what is needed."

"How long before he dies of thirst?" asked the steward.

"Asira and I discussed that concern while we prepared these oils. Some would be absorbed by the skin of a cupped hand, but not enough. If we turn him on his side, the tiniest amounts can be placed in his mouth to be swallowed or absorbed there."

"He will choke!" the steward objected

"I will not allow that to happen," said Della. The servant returned with a brimming bowl and a cup of honey.

"Enough of the oils for the moment, Thalassai." Della poured some of the honey into the water then instructed the servant to help her turn the king onto his side. When they had Kratos settled with his head pillowed on his arm, Della brought out the smallest spoon that Thalassai had ever seen.

Della smiled. "A larger spoon would be tempting. With this one, I will part his lips and let the smallest trickle of water into his mouth. With patience, we can provide enough to keep him alive. For the moment."

"How long will he sleep?" demanded the steward.

"Until he wakes," said Della. "How to waken him is the question Asira takes to the other priestesses. How do we get you to open your eyes, King of Ephyra?" she whispered softly as she poured a few drops of sweetened water between the king's lips.

***

When Della had given the king as much liquid as she felt safe providing, she helped the servants roll him onto his other side. "We must keep moving him so that he does not develop sores from pressure on one spot." When they had him settled again, she rubbed her shoulder. "I am too old for this kind of care."

"Someone else could have come to help," said Thalassai.

Della shook her head. "Even among the people of the shrine, we are limiting who knows of this illness. With the one prince wandering and the other in danger in Corfu, we do not want to spark more anxiety among the people."

The steward folded his arms. "We cannot keep the news from the city nobles forever."

"Not forever," said Della. "For today." She looked over at Thalassai. "And for the moment, you have had enough time inside. You are looking pale and tired. Take some time in the air and sun."

"I would not mind stretching my limbs," said Thalassai. A longing for freedom from the heaviness of the room took over.

"Go, dear. Absorb some sunlight. I will be here when you come back."

Thalassai hesitated. Della offered a temporary relief, not an escape from duty. For a moment, she wished she could leave the palace, return to the shrine, or better yet go home to Tiryns. She took a deep breath. "A handspan will be enough, for I am sure duties await you at the shrine."

Della smiled gently. "Take the time you need," she said as she sat cross-legged by the king and opened the stimulant jar to anoint him again.

Thalassai did not want to face questions so instead of heading to the courtyard, she asked the guard at the door for directions to the garden she had visited when she first arrived. Once outside, she raised her face to the sun. Bathed in the heat of the sun at its zenith, she felt as if all the sickness of the king's room burned away from her skin. She breathed deep the complex scents of earth and growing things.

Early spring flowers lined the path and the rich green leaves of those that would bloom in mid-summer refreshed her eyes. She wandered randomly, then caught the scent of thyme. This was where Dorlas had picked the fragrant blue flowers for her hair. Among these plants, she saw several spikes of tiny red flowers. "I know you," she said. "You are sorrel, and I think you are good for bringing down fever."

Thalassai smiled with surprise. Della's teaching had remained with her. She looked around and saw a patch of sorrel a little way down the garden. "So you are an intruder here." She bent down and carefully pulled out the weeds without disturbing the thyme's roots. The sorrel smelled sharp and fresh. She wandered down to the place where it belonged and wondered if she should transplant what she had pulled.

Beside the sorrel plants, she saw a small patch of bright green leaves grouped in fours around a cluster of deep red flowers. Near that center, the leaves were dark as if the color of the flower bled into them. She remembered this unusual plant. Melanion had brought some back from his time training with the great centaur Cheiron. He had told her its name was ateleas, meaning eternal. She had joked that it might take over the garden if it would never die out. Melanion had frowned at the joke. He told her it was a valuable herb, an important antidote.

A treatment for coma! That was what he had told her. Was it the leaves or the flowers? Or maybe it was the root. Thalassai could not remember. Probably Melanion had not shared that detail with her since medical care was not something she was interested in then.

Thalassai carefully picked one sprig of the plant. She would take this to Della, ask if she knew its properties. Perhaps they had already added it to their oils and ointments. But she had not seen it in the shrine's garden, at least that she remembered, and even in this rich garden, there was not a great deal of the eternal ateleas.

Thalassai stood. If Della did not know the plant, Asira could ask Eurynome or consult the other priestesses. Maybe it was nothing, but she hurried from the garden and back to the room where the king lay in what would be an eternal sleep if they could not find a way to waken him.

Chapter Sixteen

Twelfth day after the full moon

"Impossible. Such a thing cannot be accomplished." The headman pointed at Brizo with the heel of the barley bread his wife had provided to break the night's fast. "What you propose would steal tools we need."

The headwoman offered Brizo a cup of steaming tea and smiled softly. She seemed more open than her husband, but it was the headman he had to convince. He explained one more time that the goddess agreed to the strategy of adding armor to the oars and rudder of the ships. This would provide a fighting chance for the sailors. "The Mother would not encourage us to do the impossible," he concluded.

"Will she help you do this?" The man shook his head. "Metal is not so abundant among us that we can spare it for you to chase a wisp of dream. And if you succeed, will you take all the metal we have for arrow heads and hoes home to increase the wealth of Ephyra?"

"We will remove the metal and return it. The men will not want the burden of the extra weight on the voyage home," said Brizo.

"We won't want it when we are hurrying back to shore to escape the beast's next attack, either," Apro added.

Brizo flashed a stern look at his companion. "When we succeed in this hunt, you'll again be able to trade the bounty of your seas for what you need from the mainland. Your isolation will be broken."

"Prince Brizo," said the headwoman, "you could pay for the metal. You brought silver or amber with you, I presume."

"Some amber to exchange for supplies," said Brizo "This

is not a trading mission."

"If you pay for what we give you, then we will buy it back when you succeed," said the headwoman. "Keep the payment if you do not."

"What if they fail and take our bronze to the bottom of the ocean? That's more likely." The headman folded his arms as if that ended the discussion.

"Then we grieve their deaths, and keep their amber." The headwoman took Brizo's empty cup and rose.

"What good is amber if we cannot trade with the mainland?"

"Husband, have done. This is the best idea we have heard. I believe the Mother will aid this prince." She laid a hand on her husband's shoulder. "Think. The goddess herself came to speak with him. And she endorsed his plan."

Brizo bit back a response to that. He did not like seeing himself as so pivotal, but he could see that this argument was swaying the headman.

"We could use the amber to trade among the villages." The headman took a bite of bread.

Brizo watched the headman chew slowly. He clenched his hands as the man seemed to ponder each bite. He released his tight fingers, told himself to be patient. This headman had to be convinced in order to persuade other villages to provide what they needed. For the moment, he pushed aside the question of how they would accomplish the task if the headman agreed.

"There's a real possibility you will take our metal to the bottom of the sea, so we cannot give it all to you. I'll see what we can spare and send runners requesting that other villages do the same." The headman stood. "You three will be laden down for the walk to your camp, but you are young."

"Strong enough for that task," said Brizo, "and I hope for the fight to come."

***

Brizo felt he had exaggerated his strength by the time he and his companions climbed the hill that overlooked their camp late that afternoon. The headwoman had taken charge of collecting metal for them and had provided six sacks as heavy as they could carry. It would not be enough, but it was a good start. If she had influence on the messengers to other villages, he believed the metal would come. Now, he just had to convince Timon that the task could be accomplished, then devise a strategy to defeat the beast. *One step at a time! At least I can assure my companions that Mother Eurynome watches over us.*

As they descended the hill, Brizo could see most of the sailors hauling wood that would be used to shape new oars, and the rest gathered in a circle around a second fire larger than the one used for cooking. A broad-chested stranger had joined the crew. Perhaps those he had sent west had returned with this man.

"Where did that ox of a man come from?" Apro asked. "We could have used his help carrying this stuff."

"Not really," said Brizo. "See how he limps as he works the fire." He suspected Apro was really complaining about the whole strategy. The sailor had objected fiercely as they climbed out of the village with the sacks of metal. Fortunately, the task had required enough of his breath that he had none to spare for objections as they walked.

"Let's see what you brought," said the man as Brizo and his companions approached.

Brizo met the eyes of the sailor he had left in charge. "And this is?"

The sailor shrugged. "He arrived as we broke our fast this morning and built up this fire. He demanded to know when you would return. She came with him." He pointed to a beautiful lithe woman by the water's edge.

Brizo set down the heavy leather sacks. "I am Brizo of Ephyra. We came to your island to deal with the shark that torments you. You are?"

"Not from the island. Now let me see what we have to work with." The man limped toward Brizo. "I have been considering this challenge since your goddess came to me at sunrise. It is a task worthy of a true smith. I doubt anyone but me could manage it." He looked into Brizo's questioning face. "I am Hephaestus, God of the Forge. Now will you show me what the villagers have provided you?"

Surprise mixed with hope crowded Brizo's thoughts. Somehow, Eurynome had convinced this Olympian to aid them. He poured out the sacks of knives, arrowheads, hoe blades and other metal implements.

The god mumbled to himself as he sorted through the material. Eventually, he straightened. "This is not enough."

"The village we visited agreed to solicit more from their neighbors. They spared what they felt they could, given the headman expects us to take it to the bottom of the ocean."

Hephaestus gave a deep rumbling laugh that reverberated through his whole chest. "Well, you might, but that will be your mistake. My armor will do its part for your ship." He turned toward the shore. "Talia!"

The woman turned, and Brizo could not help but stare. Her face was perfectly shaped and her walk incredibly graceful. A nymph, he realized.

"There is a good bit of tin here and just enough copper," said Hephaestus to Brizo. "Assuming what the other villages send is similar, there are some minerals I would like to add." He turned to the nymph and his face became gentle, almost handsome. "Talia, would you help these men find the rocks we talked about?"

"Of course," said Talia. "I am sure the prince will choose companions to help me find what you need."

"I will accompany you myself, and Apro can come too." Brizo thought it would be good to keep the skeptical sailor busy, and Talia might help convince him.

"Two more to carry what I need. Now, you two build a tripod to hold my cauldron, and we'll see what I can brew up."

The two sailors Hephaestus indicated looked to Brizo, who nodded his assent. He looked for Timon and called him over. "This is Hephaestus, God of Smiths. He requires your help. Learn what you can from him."

The god turned to the terrified young man. "I don't bite. Now, bring me the long knives first."

Timon hesitated, but Brizo motioned him to do as the

Smith asked. "We will all work with you and with those of the island who join us. We must defeat this shark."

"That is your business," said Hephaestus. "Go find what I need."

Chapter Seventeen

Twelfth day after the full moon

With the white mare on one side and the chestnut stallion on the other, the black horse pounded the hard dirt of the road. A handspan earlier, Melanion had led the way from the narrow path that ran along the gulf to join the wide road south from Thebes. Now they could race forward. Several times, they passed merchants who moved their carts aside for the three. Melanion caught some nervous glances from traders who feared that racing horses meant bandits.

The horses climbed a gentle rise, and from the top they saw the landing where six boats rested. Workers prepared two sets of the rollers they used to haul ships across the narrow isthmus that separated this gulf from the eastern ocean. The oxen they used to pull the load waited patiently in harness.

Corinth charged heavily for hauling boats across the land-bridge, but because it saved the six days it took to sail all the way around, many were prepared to pay. For those who traveled inland, local merchants kept donkeys and carts to carry goods into Corinth or to more distant cities. They carried the king's seal, a sign that they were authorized and trustworthy. Corinth did what it could to secure the trade routes that were the foundation of its wealth.

Melanion slowed his horse to a walk. He studied the ships. The flags on three hung limp, so beyond recognizing the green that was common to several cities, he could not tell where they came from. The masts of three were empty just as Aphoron's had been. A cluster of tents had been thrown up on the high ground. Men milled among them, possibly

Aphoron's. He would need to be careful how he sought information. He did not want news that he followed to reach the prince.

"So what is our story?" Dermios asked.

"Thanks to your horses, you look like you are from Thessaly," said Panacea. "With that four day growth of beard, no one will know you, Melanion." She turned to Dermios. "The captain may recognize me as one of the priestesses from the shrine."

"We met at the oracle of Delphi." Melanion saw Panacea tilt her head, considering. "We represent a village on the plain near there. We visited the oracle for a blessing before coming south to seek new markets for our grain."

"When I learned you traveled south, I arranged to travel with you. Should work," said Panacea. "No one asks too many questions about the oracle."

"I seem to remember you can act proud, too," said Dermios. "You could just take the lead."

"You have come to care for me," Panacea said. "You would never have invited me to step ahead of you before the full moon."

"No sparks between you two." Melanion rubbed the neck of the stallion, willing himself to relax. "Rumors take off like gulls, and stories about strangers move quickly. Let us see what we can learn without asking too many questions."

The Corinthian captain stood with folded arms watching the workers haul one of the ships onto the rollers that would carry it across to the eastern gulf. He met them on the road looking carefully over their horses, and them.

The captain studied Panacea. "I believe I have seen you before. You serve at one of the temples."

"I return to the shrine of the God of Healing just outside the city." Panacea acknowledged the captain's bow. "These two good men agreed to escort me home from Delphi."

The captain examined Melanion and Dermios. "And then you head for home?"

"We are on our way to Corinth," said Melanion. "We represent a village of grain farmers. Our harvest has been abundant the past two years, and we are looking for new

112

markets."

"Such negotiations will take time. I recommend you stay at the Inn of the Centaur while you are in the city." The captain turned back to Panacea. "Good you don't travel this road alone, Priestess. There is a company of soldiers on the road. The captain of those three boats claimed to be a merchant but has little to trade that I can see and too many sailors. I allowed him only one quarter of his companions for his time in the city."

"Wise of you, Captain," said Panacea.

"Also called for an increase in my contingent for this night." He glanced over at the tents where men played dice and talked, a small group fished, and others returned to the makeshift camp with armloads of wood. "Too many idle soldiers here for my taste, though I heard him order two ships to head out in the morning."

"Interesting," said Panacea. "I wonder where he sent them."

"Our soldiers will be on the watch for them," said the captain. "I sent those who will enter the city to the Inn of the Centaur as well."

Panacea smiled at the captain. "Again, a wise choice for such travelers."

The man stood a little taller. "It's my job to ensure security here at the port and on the road to Corinth."

"And to oversee the work here," said Panacea, "so I leave you to the tasks at hand with the goddess' blessing." She snaked her hand in front of the captain. "May the Mother ensure that none of the trouble you foresee comes to pass."

"The goddess may guide," said the captain, "but the king's fist will be clenched and heavy if any of these strangers make trouble."

***

They stopped where a narrow path left the road. Panacea would take this up to the shrine while Melanion and Dermios continued on to Corinth.

"I will tell the high priestess Echidna what we know,"

said Panacea, "and seek her wisdom."

"You've a long story for her," said Melanion. "We'll talk as little as possible in the city."

"Time enough for the long version when we get home. I look forward to telling Melanion's little brother the whole thing," said Dermios. "Can't wait to scare him with my description of Hades."

"I only hope there will be idle time for telling tales when we arrive." Melanion shifted on his stallion's back.

"You were sent to the Inn of the Centaur because it is kept by a former soldier who still serves the king," Panacea said. "He is the king's ear among the traders. Be careful with him. May the Mother keep your mouth from irony, Dermios," said Panacea, "and watch over you both." She turned her mare up the hill and trotted out of sight.

"Easier to be discreet when you don't travel with a flashy priestess whom everybody seems to know," said Dermios.

"Everybody will know who you are when we get back to Tiryns," said Melanion.

"I suppose, though we have traveled so far I hardly know myself." Dermios smiled broadly. "And you don't look anything like the clean-shaven prince of Tiryns I've known for years."

Melanion laughed, and Dermios nudged his chestnut into a canter. The black followed an instant later, then took the lead. Melanion appreciated the fresh wind pushing through his hair. He leaned against the neck of his stallion and whispered. The stallion shifted to a gallop, and the chestnut leaped to keep up.

They did not race for long. Soon, Melanion could see the towering limestone outcrop that sheltered Corinth. At its summit, the pillars of the temple to Aphrodite gleamed in the afternoon sun. They slowed to a trot as the road brought them up to the gate into the city. Ten soldiers stood guard. Melanion and Dermios dismounted.

"Where are you from, and where are you going?" the captain of the guard demanded.

"We represent a village in Thessaly, near Delphi," said Melanion. "We come to discuss trade in barley."

The soldier looked them over carefully. "The merchants who trade for the king are not hard to find, but lodging is. A company of strangers just came in, as well as caravans from Athens and Mycenae. There may be room in the cheaper lodgings for laborers, but watch yourself there if you carry amber or silver." The soldier put a hand on the black's nose, and the stallion shook his head and backed away. "In my dreams, I ride a horse like you, but never in this life. Stabling is east of the gate. One of my companions will lead you."

Melanion accepted the guide, though he knew the way well from other visits to the city. At the stable, he negotiated with the master for the hay, and in honor of the Thessalian stallions, the man brought one the previous year's apples for each of them. The fruit was shriveled, but still a treat for the horses.

While Dermios drew water, Melanion carefully checked the hooves of both. Anxious as he was to find information on Aphoron, the horses needed attention. The journey was not yet done. He smiled. Panacea would have chided them for pushing the stallions if she were here. The criticism was a habit now, though it had an angry edge at their first meeting. She knew how much love there was between Melanion and his horse.

"These stallions are magnificent." The stable master ran a hand across the chestnut's back. The horse flicked his ear backward, but allowed the man's attention. "The plains of Thessaly produce the best mounts in our land."

"They are good companions, alert to all that goes on around us. An advantage when traveling in a new land," Melanion said. "They will appreciate your care."

The stable master gave them directions to the inn, though Melanion knew the way. Normally, he was welcomed at the palace, but he had twice stayed at the inn when he traveled to Corinth in secret, seeking information not readily shared with the prince of a rival city.

Dermios rolled his shoulders. "Do we hope for a place to sleep here, or for a night at the shrine? If we get the information we need, I will be happy to head up the hill."

Melanion half-smiled at his companion. "Without the

115

information about Aphoron's intentions..."

"We aren't going anywhere, I know."

As they approached the door of the inn, a servant boy hurried down the lane toward them with two baskets brimming with bread. "Wait, and I'll get the master for you," he said as he ducked inside the door.

Dermios tapped his foot. "Guess that's not an invitation to go in and look for Aphoron," he whispered.

Garbled voices came from the crowded common room. Someone called loudly, demanding a servant bring food. Melanion thought the voice could belong to Aphoron.

"Patience, good man. We'll feed you well as soon as we are able," said the innkeeper, a large man with the strong arms of a smith but the ruddy complexion of one who ate well. He stepped out the door and looked Melanion and Dermios over. "This must be high tide for travelers, so many have been brought to my door. I really don't have a corner tonight. Tomorrow, I'll have space. The crew that arrived today heads to Mycenae then." He rubbed his chin. "Hate to send you to the houses for laborers, but truly, I have no space."

"We were offered lodging at the shrine as thanks for escorting a priestess south from Delphi," said Melanion, "though we would rather be in the city, for we need to meet with those who manage trade for the king."

The innkeeper put his hands on his hips. "Aphrodite's' temple can be an interesting place for a man to visit."

Melanion shook his head. "This priestess belongs to a shrine in the forest."

"Know the one you mean. They serve the God of Healing there," said the innkeeper. "You will get sleep and good food. Less interesting than the temple of the Goddess of Love, though."

A bark of laughter came from the corner of the room. Melanion heard Aphoron's voice above the din, but he could not make out the words. "Wine!" one of the other sailors called. "Meat and bread," cried a third.

"Fortunately, they stay just this one night." A rumble of anger vibrated in the man's chest. "I'll see these foreigners to the city gate myself. I'll be glad to see the back of the leader of that crew. I have a runner ready to bring soldiers from the guardhouse if they get out of hand tonight. There is a wildness about them."

"We'll happily stay clear of any trouble these visitors bring." Melanion bowed his head.

"Until tomorrow then." The man turned back to the crowded room and called for a servant.

"So it's the shrine for us, along with the snakes they keep." Dermios spoke softly as they made their way back to the stable. "As long as we get there before dark, or we'll have a lonely night in the forest."

"The stallions will get us there." Melanion frowned. "Why is Aphoron going to Mycenae?"

Chapter Eighteen

Twelfth day after the full moon

Della and a servant rolled the king from his back onto his side. When they had arranged the light woolen sheet over him, Thalassai sat down to study his face. Nothing had changed. No movement of eyelid or lip to show he was even dreaming. His chest rose and fell slowly, his breathing shallow. *How long can this go on?* she wondered.

Though the king's condition had not changed, Thalassai felt as if everything else had. When she had made the journey to the river's birthplace, she could not have imagined her new role in the palace or at the king's side. Suddenly, she remembered the promise she had made that morning, the promise to return to the shrine, visit, and perhaps share in their work. She had seen so much of Della and the priestess she had forgotten.

Selene slipped into the room. She handed Della the basket she carried and a small jar. "Asira sent finely ground herbs to place under his tongue."

"Is that the ateleas I found this morning?" Thalassai asked.

"Asira thanks you for the herb, but is not yet sure what part of it to use. This is a mix of basil, laurel, and garlic oil." Selene sat beside the king. "He is the same?"

"No change," Della said. "This mixture is an effective stimulant when swallowed. Which he cannot do. I trust it will do some good when applied as Asira suggests under his tongue." She unpacked the basket.

"Della," said Thalassai tentatively. "I promised to return to the shrine. The day I went to the river's birthplace, I mean.

Should I make that visit?"

Della placed herbs in a small bowl and began to grind them with a pestle. "What should you do? A very good question. With Selene to assist me, you are not needed here for the moment."

Della focused on her work for so long that Thalassai wondered if she had forgotten the question.

"The market," Della said. "Take a walk in the market; look positive. It will do the city good to see you. You don't want too many questions though, so is there someone other than a servant who can accompany you?"

"I met a young woman, Preema, at the banquet. She might walk with me."

"Perfect." Della looked to the servants. "Would one of you request her presence? Tell her she is to dress to accompany the princess on an afternoon walk."

One of the servants stepped forward hesitantly, but Thalassai nodded to him to confirm the request. "If she is available, tell her I will meet her in the courtyard."

***

Thalassai stood in the doorway of the palace. She folded her hands and held them still, though her thoughts wandered. She did not wait long.

"I am honored that you asked me to walk with you," Preema said. She had her hair loosely braided and wore a brown robe with bronze clasps at the shoulders. "Is there a part of town that you would like especially to see?"

Thalassai stepped toward the girl. "I enjoyed the market, and it is good to hear from the farmers." A thought came to her, and she smiled. "I have not been to the weavers' street though, and you might show me the ones your family is patron of."

"I will introduce you to them and to the best cloth maker in Ephyra, and then we can go to the produce market." Preema glanced at her bodyguard and at the Ephyran soldier whom the steward had assigned to accompany them. "I am not used to the company of soldiers when I go out."

"They will walk ahead and behind," said Thalassai, "so we are free to talk."

As they walked the road outside the palace gate, Preema chatted about the people who lived in each house, telling Thalassai where their farms were, what crafters they were patrons of, how the families got along. Thalassai listened carefully, trying to map out the web of relationships in this city. These were things she knew about Tiryns. It was useful to know who always argued with whom.

At the weavers' street, Thalassai was surprised that Preema led her to one of the smaller shops. The two soldiers remained outside, and Preema introduced her to the weaver. The woman brought out samples of woolen cloth.

"This is as fine a weave as I have ever seen," Thalassai exclaimed.

"Thank you, Princess. My oldest son is the spinner, and he is meticulous." The weaver spread one of the lengths. "And my husband is very choosey about the fleeces we use."

"Their linen is also lovely," said Preema. "You must visit here in the fall after the flax is harvested."

The shopkeeper smiled and bowed to them. Outside, Thalassai looked down the street to the other weaving shops. "Is that the family that you are patron of?"

"No. Those weavers are so skilled that they remain independent. Come and I will introduce you to the one my family has taken on."

The two soldiers followed as Preema led the way to another shop farther down the lane. The shopkeeper looked nervous when he bowed to Preema. She reassured him that she was not there to check on the work but to introduce the princess to merchants in the city. The man then proudly brought out samples of woolen cloaks.

"The work is admirable, "said Thalassai, "and the shade of dye is quite unusual."

"The recipe has been a secret of our family for two generations, Princess. It is one of the reasons we attracted such a powerful sponsor."

Thalassai wanted to roll her eyes at such obvious stroking of the patron's ego, but she kept the thought from showing on her face. She and Preema left to make their way to the market.

Thalassai appreciated Della's suggestion that she take Preema with her. It was lovely to relax with a companion almost her own age. Preema seemed to enjoy the time as well, as they examined produce and listened to farmers rejoice in the fact that the river was full. They had almost completed their circuit when Thalassai saw the steward rush into the square trailed by two soldiers.

"Something has disturbed him," said Preema quietly, a frown creasing her forehead.

As he hurried toward them, Thalassai held up her hand so that he would not blurt out in public the issue that troubled him. "It is kind of you to come yourself to escort us back to the palace, Steward." She met his eyes and raised her eyebrows, willing him to smile and bow. When he did, she continued. "We must escort Preema to her home on the way to the palace."

"Of course." The steward fell into step beside Thalassai as they crossed the square. Once in the empty street, he spoke quietly and urgently. "There is a dispute about loading the ship from Paxos. Two merchants are in the king's hall ready to knife each other."

"Who is it, and why do they argue?" Thalassai asked.

When the steward named them, Preema laughed. "Those two are cousins who are always competing with each other. They never actually battle, but they threaten each other all the time. Why did the king not silence them?"

Thalassai appreciated the information, but wondered how to answer her companion's question. She decided that it was better to say something about the king's condition rather than have her imagine worse. *What speculation could be worse than the truth,* she thought, then pushed that worry away. "We do not want the news to spread across the city, but the king is ill and confined to his rooms today. I will deal with these two. What do they ship?"

"One is sending eight full-grown rams, and the other, urns to store olive oil," the steward said. "They cannot really be loaded on the same ship, and both want their merchandise on this boat."

Thalassai cast her mind back to the night of the banquet and recited to herself as much of the conversation as she could remember. *They lost several male sheep to an illness in the winter, and the ewes are ready to breed.* She also remembered that the island was short of transport because of the tidal waves. "Urns won't be used until the fall harvest. This is a simple matter of what is most needed on the island." Then another thought came. "Could we spare a ship of our own, Steward?"

He thought for a moment. "I believe we could make one available the day after tomorrow."

"Then, I will tell them that the rams will be shipped tomorrow, but the king will provide transport for the urns later. Our ship can return with the fish and fruit promised us."

"A good plan, Princess. And I believe you can convince them of it."

Thalassai saw his shoulders ease and his face relax. If he believed she could manage this, convincing the merchants should not be difficult at all.

Chapter Nineteen

Twelfth night after the full moon

A young girl lit oil lamps around the room while another brought a tray with cups of tea to the priestess Echidna, to Dermios, and to Panacea. Melanion declined the one he was offered and continued to pace back and forth across the room. Panacea cradled her cup in her hands, breathed in the fragrant mixture, frowned at the prince whose worry she shared.

"Why would Aphoron go to Mycenae?" she asked. "Your father has strong ties with King Atreus and his city, does he not?"

"Had. Last time I met with their ambassador, he told me King Atreus has increased the size of his army, implied he wants better access to our port." *That was the same day Aphoron kidnapped my sister.* Melanion went to the open window, leaned both hands on the stone. "I must find a way to follow Aphoron and uncover his plans."

"I do not think that your path runs west." Echidna's fingers played rhythmically against the side of her cup. "The message from Panacea's father said danger threatens your city and Ephyra. The northern city cannot be your concern, but your own city is. I believe you need to go directly there."

Melanion gripped the window ledge hard. His sister was in one of the storm centers and beyond his reach. If he went south while Aphoron traveled west, the prince would be out of his reach as well. If only he was like the gods who could flit from one place to another. But he was human, trapped in a body that could only put one foot in front of the other. And unlike the god who had sent the message with the owl, he could only see what was right in front of him. He clenched his hands. "What does your father know that we do not, Panacea?"

"Because he is a healer, many visit him. He senses currents that others do not," she said. "What we know is that Aphoron is ambitious and has a taste for revenge."

"What revenge will he find against Melanion in Mycenae?" Dermios asked.

"Melanion." Echidna waited until the prince turned toward her. "A traveler from the south said that the earth has shaken five times in the valley where Tiryns sits. Why would Poseidon shake the foundations of your city?"

Panacea sat straight, set her cup down. "Mel, you said that a tribe of Cyclopes built the walls of Tiryns. What if Poseidon's son, the cyclops Aphoron visited, was one of the builders? What if he knows a secret about the wall?"

"What kind of secret could the giant know?" Dermios sounded skeptical.

"And would they betray the memory of my grandfather when building the walls was a gift to honor him?" asked Melanion.

"As I have said before, any creatures sired by Poseidon are bound to serve their father's desires," said Panacea.

Melanion turned back to stare out into the dark yard of the shrine. Lantern light spilled onto the grounds from several windows, creating eerie shadows, hiding as much as illuminating. The bits and pieces they learned about Aphoron's plans were like that, showing hints but hiding the overall intention. *The Earthshaker isn't going to show me what he's up to. I just have to figure it out.*

Suddenly, like an arrow striking the center of a target, the information Echidna provided slid into place. He knew what the Earthshaker had done. He sent a prayer to Mother Eurynome to look after his sister and turned back to the room. "I believe that Aphoron will tell Atreus that the wall can be breached. The king of Mycenae will send an army south to take my city. He gets a port; Aphoron gets revenge; Poseidon makes me pay and gains the homage of Mycenae."

"There are other plots in play," said Echidna, "but I

believe you read his intentions for your city correctly. You must go home."

"What will Aphoron do once the message is delivered to the Mycenaen king?" Dermios asked. "What if he heads out to raid villages up and down the coast? What if he really heads to Sparta? He's a snake as well as a pig, with my apologies to our hostess for disparaging the creatures she honors, with this comparison."

"I suspect he will want to see the fruit of revenge first hand, but we cannot know for sure." Melanion frowned deeply. "Wherever he goes, we must get ahead of him and prepare Tiryns for an assault."

"I could go to Mycenae," said Panacea. Melanion started to object, but she lifted a hand to stop him. "Don't say it isn't my task. The villages on this coast are under our protection, and raids here would be our business."

"Are you certain?" Melanion asked. "It may be dangerous."

Panacea laughed. "Not as dangerous as traveling with you has been." She smiled sadly. "Less dangerous than heading for a city about to be stormed by the army of Mycenae."

"I agree with your proposal, Panacea," said Echidna. "I will send you with a message for the priestess of Artemis in that city, a reason for your travel. There you can verify Aphoron's next step and check if we have guessed correctly about what Atreus will do."

Melanion folded his arms. He felt calmer. He did not have the foresight of a god, but he could follow the logic he saw. The next stage of his journey was clear. "Dermios, we leave for home at dawn."

Chapter Twenty

Twelfth night and thirteenth day after the full moon

A young girl ran into the dining hall of the shrine of Eurynome. Conversation stopped as the out-of-breath child knelt in front of Asira. "Priestess," she said, "The link! You are summoned!"

Asira placed a gentle hand on the girl's shoulder. The child trembled. This would have been the first time she was in the sanctuary when the summoning happened. "Remain and take your dinner," she said to the young one.

As she got to her feet, the priestess made her face calm, though she heard curiosity and worry among her people as she walked from the dining hall.

Asira's thoughts raced ahead of her footsteps as she entered the narrow stone hallway. The turnings of the labyrinth should have calmed her mind, but worry nagged at her like the undertow of waves that crashed against rocks. She had intended to use the link to request help from the priestesses of the Mother, but clearly there was another problem at one of the other shrines. *Too much trouble already, and now what is happening? Mother help us!*

At the base of the steep stairs into the sanctuary, four lamps burned in the stone hall. Soft light like the shining of a quarter moon came from the long crack in the wall, the sign of summoning.

She pushed her worries to the back of her mind, calmed her breathing, and prepared to link with the other priestesses. She placed her hand on the cold stone. An instant later, warmth flooded into her.

I am here, she said in her mind.

It is I, Lipela, who called. There is trouble in the city near our shrine.

Asira wondered what had happened in the city of Didome. *I was coming to the link myself this night. More trouble in our valley.*

Who summoned us? The senior priestess, Pheggas, entered the link.

Lipela's mind voice was quiet as she answered, *I did.*

Asira was surprised at the impatience in Pheggas' mind-voice. The senior priestess had been rebuked by Mother Eurynome the night of the red full moon, but instead of learning to honor her fellow priestesses, Pheggas seemed more irritated than ever.

All are here? Pheggas asked. When only Asira and Lipela answered, anger crept into her mind voice. *We wait for the fourth. I tell my story only once.*

Concern mounted in Asira. A problem had arisen for Pheggas as well.

I am sorry I am late, said Timandra, the priestess of the fourth shrine. *I just returned from the palace. The king of the city here has fallen into a strange sleep, and the palace called on me to attend him.*

The king here sleeps as well! said Asira. *What power is at work?*

The coma of our king is the reason I summoned you, said Lipela. *I can give him a little water, but nothing else. What could have caused such an illness?*

Silence filled the link before Pheggas spoke. Her mind-voice was quiet now but urgent. *The king of the nearest city to us also sleeps. I received the message this morning. I have not examined him myself, so describe the condition for me.*

Asira listened while Lipela described exactly the same kind of sleep that held King Kratos. Lipela described the treatments she had attempted.

I have provided essential salts through a skin ointment, Asira said. *Today a visitor to our valley said she thought that ateleas might treat coma, but I do not know what part of the plant to use or how to prepare it.*

I have heard that the centaurs use it, said Timandra, *but I do not know how.*

I think we must discover who caused this, said Lipela.

You mean what *has caused this,* said Pheggas. *We will ask Eurynome that question.*

Asira took a deep breath. At the full moon, Eurynome had chided her for not standing up to Pheggas. She would not make the same mistake again so soon, though she expected the senior priestess would make her pay for arguing with her. *Pheggas, wait. It is clearly not an illness but an attack.* Asira sensed cold anger from the priestess but continued despite it. *We might ask* who *caused this, but the urgent question is how to waken the kings, or at least how to keep them alive until they waken on their own.*

'How should we care for the kings?' would be my question, said Timandra. *That way the Mother can tell us how to treat them, how to waken them, and how to challenge whoever initiated this attack if that would assist us.*

Asira sent her agreement into the link and sensed the same from Lipela. Pheggas hesitated, hiding her thoughts from the others. Surely, she would see the wisdom of this question.

If you insist, said Pheggas, *we will pose this question to the Mother and see what happens. Together then.*

The senior priestess sounded both irritated and smug. If Eurynome chided them in any way, Pheggas would use this to strengthen her position. Deep in her mind, away from the link, Asira prayed for the goddess to tell them all they needed to know whether they asked the best question or not. Then, she joined her thoughts to the others', to call the goddess and ask how to care for the four comatose kings.

My daughters. The voice of Eurynome came among them with warmth and sheltering peace. *I have been chasing Poseidon's other plans, and only yesterday received news of the kings' sleep. I spent this day with the God of Healing. Attend to the kings in the morning, and I will come to you to waken them.*

Are there herbs you need, or a fire? asked Pheggas.

Ateleas, if you have it, the goddess answered.

There is a little of the herb here in Ephyra, said Asira.

Bring fresh leaves picked that morning to Kratos. The God of

Healing has provided enough of the herb for the others.

We have given the king water, honey, and stimulant oils, said Lipela. *Can we do anything more this night?*

Rest, said Eurynome. *This is a spell of the Olympian Hypnos who has served Poseidon in the past. There was no way you could waken them. I will visit each king as the sun rises into the sky.*

The link ended, and Asira removed her hand from the wall. Poseidon again!

***

Dorlas woke Thalassai before dawn with news that Asira had summoned her to the king's bedside. As she rose, Thalassai wondered what had changed. "A simple knee-length robe, please. And a shawl for warmth."

As soon as Dorlas braided her hair, Thalassai took a small oil lamp to light her way to the king's chambers. Four lamps burned in the room to chase the gloom of illness. The king's personal servant massaged his hands with a fragrant oil, but the king's face showed no sign that he felt anything.

Mother, despite his betrayal this past season, Thalassai prayed, *this too is your child. Come and help him.*

Thalassai felt blanketed by a gentle warmth. *I am coming, Daughter,* was all the goddess said.

I will try to be patient until you arrive, Thalassai thought. She went to the east-facing window. The sky outside shifted from black to burnished bronze. As the moon slipped into the sky, the fine crescent shone red. Like a tilted bowl, it seemed to pour a stream of wine toward the rising sun.

What is this? Thalassai prayed. The dawn moon only shone red before winter storms. *We need peace, Mother!*

The door opened, and Asira entered with the steward. Thalassai thought the lines of worry on her face had grown deeper overnight. She carried freshly picked ateleas. Pride made Thalassai smile. Her recognition of the herb had been a good thing! She looked down at the motionless king and her smile faded.

Asira examined him. "He sleeps as deeply as ever," she said. "You should also know that three other kings also sleep."

"That is why the moon pours out the red light of mourning," Thalassai whispered.

"I saw the moon as I left the garden. Remember that we pour the first wine of autumn on the ground as an offering of gratitude. See, as the sun rises, it shines bright as silver." Asira came and stood beside Thalassai. "Eurynome comes with the sun to waken him."

Thalassai turned back to the window. A shaft of clear light shot from behind the mountains and touched the thin crescent chasing away the red stain. "There will be no storm today? The Mother promises health?" she asked.

Asira went to the window to study the sky. "I believe you read the sign aright."

Thalassai thought that worry filled the spaces between her words even though the priestess' voice was quiet and confident. The news that this same sleep had taken three other kings troubled her deeply. "Did the Mother tell you what has happened to them?"

"The Olympian Hypnos caused this unnatural sleep."

"What has Hypnos to gain from this?" asked the steward.

"Tales claim that he has worked with Poseidon in the past." Asira knelt beside the king and laid her hand on his forehead. He did not move. Her frown deepened.

"Will the Mother come here first?" Thalassai asked. Asira shook her head, and Thalassai wondered if that meant she did not know, or that it did not matter.

Thalassai watched the sky slowly brighten. She made herself breathe steadily and slowly as she waited for the goddess. She glanced at the steward, who paced back and forth across the room with his hands clasped behind his back and his eyes on the floor. His lips moved, but he did not speak aloud. She wondered what conversation he was having with himself.

Warmth like afternoon in a walled garden flooded the room. Eurynome appeared beside Asira, kneeling by the king. "Steward, I need a wooden box," the goddess commanded.

The man bit his lip and then signaled to one of the

servants who hurried from the room. "You must waken him quickly," he said.

"I will lift the veil of sleep that has been placed on him," Eurynome said, "when you get me that box." She touched the king's cheek. Only his lips moved, curving slightly into a weak smile. "This is the deepest sleep of the four."

"You have wakened the others?" Asira asked.

The goddess nodded. "They are weak, but they will recover physically. They are greatly disturbed, however. Dreams troubled their minds while they slept."

Thalassai looked up from the king. She heard sadness in Eurynome's voice, and she read concern in the creases beside her eyes. The recovery of the kings left the goddess with a problem, but Thalassai could not yet place what it was.

"Kratos," Eurynome said softly. "Time to wake up." She took the leaves of ateleas from Asira and crushed them in her hands. A fresh scent brightened the whole room. She held the bruised plant where the king could breathe in the fragrance.

Thalassai felt hope as the king shifted slightly on the rug, but he settled again. Fear gripped her heart. What if Eurynome could not waken this king?

A servant rushed in with a small wooden box. Eurynome took it and placed it open on the floor. Then she brushed a gentle hand from the top of the king's head to his chin. Thalassai thought she saw the glimmer of a veil, finer than any cloth, cling to the goddess' hand. The goddess moved her hand to the box and folded the glimmer inside. She closed the lid.

Kratos opened his eyes. He tried to sit up, but his arm gave way. He glared at those who knelt by his bed. "What are you all doing in my room? Steward, explain."

"You slept, my dear," said Eurynome.

Kratos raised his hand, and the steward helped him to sit. "That is what night is for," he objected.

"You slept for three nights and two days, my king," said the steward. "We were deeply worried."

"I could not have slept so long." Kratos allowed his

steward to help him to his feet as the others stood as well.

"It was not a natural sleep," said Eurynome. "What did you dream?"

"I dreamed that my kingdom had strengthened, that the kings of the south bowed to me. Then..." Kratos frowned.

Eurynome watched his face for a moment. "Then you dreamed that the Olympians acknowledged your power, I presume."

When the king folded his arms, Thalassai thought that the goddess had guessed correctly, but Kratos did not want to acknowledge that he had believed the dream.

"Why did I sleep as long as you say?" The king looked at Eurynome with an accusation in his eyes.

The goddess answered quietly, calmly. "It was a spell laid by the Olympian Hypnos."

Kratos' eyes went wide for a moment, then he hid his surprise. "At whose bidding?"

The lines around Eurynome's eyes creased into a smile that did not touch her lips. "I believe Poseidon arranged this."

Kratos turned to his steward. "Prepare me food and then a bath. I must clean the residue of this spell from my body."

"Make it a light meal of broth," said Asira. "And you need to move, release the build-up inside your body. A stroll in the city would reassure the people, though you will not be able to go a great distance. You will find that the illness weakened you."

"The magic, you mean." Kratos folded his arms and glared at the priestess. "I must ponder this news, but tomorrow we will call an assembly of the leading citizens. Poseidon has proved he is powerful and determined."

"But the Mother woke you," said Thalassai. A wave of nausea rose in her stomach. If the king returned to Poseidon, she would run from the city. She wanted nothing to do with that ambitious, arrogant god.

"And Poseidon could just as quickly put me to sleep again," said the king. "Your power wanes, Eurynome. The Olympians rise."

"Your dreams told you that, dreams designed by an

132

Olympian?" Eurynome's voice was quiet but there was a hard edge to it as well.

Thalassai struggled to think clearly. "King Kratos, you cannot let Poseidon bully you into worshipping him. We know he is fickle. You cannot depend on him."

"I can't seem to depend on the goddess either," said Kratos. "Something must be done to stop these catastrophes."

"I agree," said Eurynome. "We must stop Poseidon's ploys. The people suffer. Recover from one and another comes. Earthshakings weaken the land in many places, and the shark your son hunts is a danger to all."

"How is Brizo, and how goes his quest?" asked Thalassai. "I have thought of him often, even as I watched the king."

Kratos did not take his eyes off the goddess. "How do you propose I deal with the god's interference in my valley?"

Eurynome picked up the box. "I ask for two days, Kratos. Only that. You need those days to recover your strength, and I believe Poseidon can be constrained in that time."

The king turned away and leaned on the window ledge breathing heavily. His hands shook where they lay on the stone ledge. "I am not strong enough for a full conclave." Finally, he turned back. "Two days. I will give you that much time. No more than that can I afford to wait."

Chapter Twenty-one

Thirteenth day after the full moon

Brizo rose before the sun, but others were already up and working. The longlines had been cleared of their catches and the cooking fire stoked. On the other side of the cove, Hephaestus leaned on his crutch as two shadowy figures banked the coals of the forge fire. One of them would be Timon. The man had not left the god's side since he was assigned the duty of assisting the Smith. Despite his initial worry, Timon excitedly absorbed everything Hephaestus taught.

Soon they would put the armor the god created to the test. At least it would not be hard to find the creature they hunted. Those who had come from the villages claimed the shark could sense the launch of a ship. None had reached more than twenty ship-lengths from shore before she hit them. Wondering if the she-shark ever slept, he turned toward the dark water and saw that the crescent moon was stained red as blood.

Brizo walked to the water's edge. The color of the moon made the hair on his neck rise. In winter, such a morning stain on moon or cloud meant storm, a warning for sailors to watch for the southern wind that carried dust, rain, and danger.

This day, though, not a wisp of cloud marred the perfect dome of the sky. Did the red light warn of some other storm that Poseidon brewed? Or did it carry another meaning? Half a moon earlier, when the full moon had risen red, the goddess had intended a message of promise. *Does this red moon mean hope or trouble?*

Brizo waited. Before long, the first ray of the sun crossed the still water to his feet and a second shot upward, turning the moon into a bright silver bowl. He breathed easier. No storms this day, and perhaps the goddess promised success for their enterprise. The work of Mother Eurynome was never simple, however, and that moment of red could also be a warning.

Brizo went to the cooking fire and got a platter of fish with bread that had been brought from one of the villages. He took it to those who worked the forge fire. Timon filled him in on their progress, assured him that the material they needed had come. Hearing the confidence in Timon's voice made Brizo feel that the armoring of the boats would be accomplished.

He returned to the other fire where Talia assisted the cooks. "Your support in our endeavor is greatly appreciated," he said to the nymph.

"My sisters chide me for my choice of husband, saying I have condemned myself to a life of drudgery amidst smoke and the tang of molten metal." She smiled, her face warm and tender as she looked toward the forge fire. "I would say to them, if they cared to listen, that I have traveled to wonderful wild places with him. Am I not here on this island where I walk among ancient trees? See those that cling to the cliffs. Do you know how old they are?"

Brizo felt a twinge of regret with this reminder that she was a tree spirit. They were burning a great deal of wood. "Would it ease your heart to have us plant trees to replace the ones we are burning?"

Talia's laughter rang like a dozen tiny bells of silver. "The princess that loves you is most fortunate. Seldom has any hero made such a gracious offer."

Brizo felt himself blush a deep red. He did not think he was a hero.

She looked across the beach toward the inland hills of the island. "The idea you present is interesting. May I take two of the men who harvested wood for your oars and rudder to retrieve seeds and seedlings?"

"I will choose two who know something about trees

to accompany you." Brizo studied the men who ate their morning meal. "As Timon is learning the skill of a smith, it will be an unexpected benefit if we return to my city with new skills in forest husbandry."

"When you return to your city," said Talia. "When you return."

***

Knowing that Hephaestus had as much help as he wanted, Brizo spent the morning working with those who shaped the new rudders. This was familiar work. With so many hidden rocks on this coast, breaking oar or rudder was not uncommon. At home, craftsmen used an adze to smooth the rudder's surface, but the chip marks left by the axes would not affect its performance.

The sun was halfway to its zenith when three men laden with metal made their way down the steep hill into the cove. Brizo studied the new arrivals. Like all the men of the island, they were rather short in stature but broad across the shoulders. Their arms were marked with scars from rope burns and fishhook cuts, but they had strong muscles. He left the woodworkers to meet them. "Thank you for the metal you contribute. Each piece moves us closer to defeating the monster."

"You are certain this will work?" the oldest of the group asked. "Even once you return the weight of metal to us, it will have to be reworked."

Brizo nodded. "With the God of the Forge directing us, we will succeed. And when the creature is dead, my companions will stay to help reshape your tools. Let us bring these to the Smith."

Hephaestus poured out the sacks one by one, sorting by some principle Brizo could not identify. He handed Timon some things to go directly to the smelting urn.

When he came upon a small metal bowl inlaid with figures, he stood straight with it resting on his palm. "Marvelous. Perfectly marvelous. This is not the work of a Grecian crafter. From farther east it comes. See, it tells a story of creation where a great monster is cut in half. And the metal." He flicked one fingernail against the rim of the bowl, and it rang like a bell. "What a precious mix they used! This we will not melt." Reverently, Hephaestus handed it back.

"This bowl has been in our village a long time. We did not know it was so valuable."

Hephaestus scowled. "The things you people take for granted. Now let me get back to work."

"You are hungry after your journey, I am certain," Brizo said to the newcomers. "If you go to the other fire, my companion will provide food."

The others crossed the beach to the cooking fire, but the one who held the bowl remained. "What are those men doing?" He pointed to the four who used hammers to split the rocks Talia had helped Brizo collect the day before.

"It seems there is a vein of material in them that the god is adding to the mix," said Brizo. "He was adamant that it would strengthen the armor."

"Will it be enough?"

"Hephaestus seems quite confident." Brizo watched the god show Timon which pieces to add to the molten mix.

The man picked up one of the stones the sailors were splitting and examined it. "Rocks like this are common here. What is the value of the seam?"

"I would not ask right at the moment," said Brizo. "Hephaestus does not seem to mind watchers, but interruptions are not appreciated."

Hephaestus spoke quietly, almost to himself. Timon leaned in, listening carefully to the mutterings of the Smith.

Suddenly, Timon stood tall and snapped his fingers. "Sand. We've all the sand we need."

"Explain," demanded Hephaestus.

"Packed sand can be used as a form, and we have a beach full of it." Timon hurried on. "We tamp it down, then press in each oar and the two rudders. Each form will fit perfectly."

"The place needs to be perfectly level," Hephaestus pointed out.

Timon thought for a moment. "We could use a bowl,

brimful of water."

Hephaestus grunted. "An adequate plan. If those woodworkers have finally completed their task, show them how to prepare the molds."

"That will only cover one side of the oar," Brizo said.

The God of Smiths scowled at him. "Given how little metal we have received and the need to hurry, that will have to do."

"But for the rudders, we must do both sides of them," said Brizo. "We can maneuver even if some of the oars are broken, but the rudder must be intact."

"I suppose you have a point," said the god. "We will do the rudders first. The armor coating on one side will have to cool before we do the second side. Get to it, Timon. The rest of you leave me to focus."

The god leaned over the urn and breathed in deeply. "Smells just about right. What I need is…" Hephaestus muttered to himself as he sorted through the pile of plow blades, knives, and cups.

Brizo smiled to the villager who still held the bowl. "We'd best leave them be." He walked away.

The man followed two steps, then stopped. He stared at the quiet waters of the bay where five of Brizo's companions carried a net into the water.

"What are they doing?" he demanded. "Stop them. Call them back." The man looked at Brizo, eyes wide, with pain written across his face. "That's why we only use longlines. The monster. It will come!"

Brizo grabbed a cutlass from the pile of metal and ran toward the shore. The soft sand held his feet so he felt like he crawled. "Back!" he shouted. The men, chest deep in the water, paused and looked over their shoulders. "Out of the water. Leave the net." Brizo kept running, scanning the water as he did. "Come!"

A huge white fin rose five ship-lengths from the men. One of them saw and shouted. They dropped the net and pushed through the water toward shore.

Brizo splashed into the waves. The shark raced toward his companions at unbelievable speed. The fin disappeared. He was two arm-lengths from them.

The fin reappeared right behind the men. One of them screamed and fell beneath the waves. The man next to him grabbed his arm and pulled his head above the surface. Both were hauled deeper. Brizo surged forward until he could see the shape of the shark. He swung the cutlass at the fin. It bounced off, but the shark thrashed, releasing the man. The water turned red, but Brizo knew this was his companion's blood, not the creature's.

"Get him to shore." Brizo slashed the long nose of the shark, who swung her head toward him. He saw the teeth, longer than his hand and sharp as the cutlass he carried. With two hands, he brought the blade down on the point of the creature's snout. It bounced. There was no mark where he had hit her snout, but the creature thrashed again.

He swung again, but she withdrew from his blade. He felt relief. Then, another thought came to him. *Can I draw her into the shallows, perhaps ground her?* He took a small step toward her, and she swam in place, mouth open, threatening.

She slashed at him with her teeth, but Brizo was out of reach. A wave rolled past, and the sand slipped beneath his feet. He was not certain that he could hold his footing, and he dared not slip. The shark did not come toward him. Instead, it swam backward, then turned aside. Brizo watched the fin cut through the water parallel to the beach and then back again. Three times the shark patrolled the cove before it headed out to deep water. Brizo returned to the shore.

Men gathered around their injured companion whose leg was gone below the knee. The sand was stained blood red, and the man had fainted. Two sailors held him still, and Hephaestus approached with a red-hot knife.

"I will cauterize the wound, or he will bleed to death." Hephaestus did not wait for Brizo to acknowledge the need. "Keep him absolutely still," he said to the men who held him.

Brizo turned back to the ocean. Hephaestus and his men knew what they were doing. He would go to the cook and order broth made for the injured sailor. Perhaps Talia had seen herbs that would aid healing while she was in the forest. At least salt water meant the wound was sterile, unlike a battle injury.

He looked out where the shark had disappeared. He had not been able to break the skin of the beast. With all his strength he had barely marked the armor of her hide. *If I cannot cut her, how can we kill her?*

Chapter Twenty-two

Thirteenth day after the full moon

The two horses climbed the last ridge, and Melanion gazed across the valley to the walled city of Tiryns, his home. Only thirteen days earlier he and Dermios had ridden this same road at a gallop, heading north. They had met Panacea that evening, and the full moon had been red that night. Again this morning, as they parted from her, the moon had been tinted the color of blood.

The priestess Echidna claimed that the red crescent spoke of promise, but to Melanion it was a clear sign that the Earthshaker was sowing trouble like barley seeds. He hoped Panacea was not riding into danger, though he and Dermios were likely riding directly toward Poseidon's target. *One of his targets,* he thought and sent a prayer to Eurynome to look after Thalassai. *Prayer is getting to be a new habit for me.* In a way the words helped push aside worry, and he'd found the goddess more reliable than the Olympians he had come across.

"The valley looks like it always has," said Dermios. "No sign of what the god and his lackey might be up to."

"You don't expect them to be obvious, do you?" Melanion glanced at his companion.

"I live in hope."

Melanion grinned. "Let us get to the city, and see what we can discover." He kneed his stallion into a gallop, and together they descended the road into the valley. He did not know if their guesses the night before were correct, but he no longer felt torn about the choice. He needed to return home.

The horses ate up the distance on the familiar road. Before

long, they came to the city wall. The guards saluted him, right fists to their hearts, as he dismounted.

Dermios swung his leg over the stallion's neck and slid off. "Last time we rode through this gate, the steward waited with news of Thalassai's kidnapping." He spoke too quietly for the guards to hear. "This time *we* bear the bad news."

"You'll want to take the stallions to the stable yourself?" asked one of the guards.

"It's on our way." Melanion thought the man might ask more, but the guards were well trained. *News and rumors will race through the city soon enough,* he thought.

At the stable, a boy was sent running to inform King Gryneus that they had returned. Servants got water for the stallions, and the head groom promised to brush them down and examine their feet himself. They left the horses in his care and headed for the palace.

The boy must have shouted the news of the prince's arrival to folks along the way, because many waited in the doorways of their homes and shops to greet them. It was not long before someone asked about Thalassai.

"She is fine, but the full story goes to my father first," Melanion said. The rest of the way, people sang out their relief that his sister was well, though as they passed, he heard some ask why the princess was not with them.

"Always amazes me, the way news travels faster than we do in this city," said Dermios.

Melanion's uncle, Broteus, met them in the courtyard in front of the palace. "Don't worry; I am not going to ask where your sister is. I can wait until we get to your father."

"She is well, but it is a long story, and other dangers are brewing. How have things been here while we were gone?"

Broteus fell into step beside Melanion. "All has been quiet except for the rumblings of the earth."

"We heard Poseidon's power had been felt here," said Melanion. "Any rumblings from our neighbors?"

"The watchers in the passes have seen nothing," Broteus said. "Still, I will be relieved when the fleet returns."

"Their sails have not been sighted?" Melanion frowned. "With the prevailing wind behind them, they should have arrived this day."

Broteus' brow creased. "Even in summer, the waters can be unpredictable. I will send word to the port to watch for their return. The news they are on the way is a comfort."

Melanion did not answer. They needed more than just news of the fleet. Given what he suspected, they needed the soldiers on patrol in the city.

Guards at the king's chamber opened the door for the three to enter. King Gryneus sat, arms crossed, on his throne on the raised dais. Melanion's younger brother ran to him and placed his hand on Melanion's chest.

"You are back," he said, "and we hear Thalassai is well." He looked past his brother. "Where is she?"

Melanion laid a hand over his brother's and smiled down at the young man. Then he looked up to meet his father's eyes. "We arrived in time to prevent the marriage of Thalassai to Poseidon." He walked forward to stand just in front of his father. "You will be proud of your daughter. She grew strong enough to challenge the plans of her captors, and with aid, she was freed."

"Then she sails with the fleet, and you rode ahead to give the news?" King Gryneus shook his head. "This is not what I read on your face."

"Thalassai remains in Ephyra for the moment," said Melanion. "We came south chasing the prince who kidnapped her. He has gone to Mycenae, and we believe he will encourage Atreus to attack here."

"That seems a strange conclusion to draw," said the king. "And why is my daughter, whom I have always been proud of, still in that traitor's city?"

"The fleet might have ended up in a battle. We did not want Thalassai in the middle of a fight after all we did to prevent that." Melanion bowed to his father. "We left one ship to guard her."

The king frowned. "That ship could have waited one or perhaps two days and then safely carried her home rather leaving her in the city of a prince who betrayed our trust."

Melanion took a deep breath. "One of our men carries her words to you, but I know the content of the message. The second prince of Ephyra, now heir to the throne, is a good man, and she will ask for your permission to marry him."

King Gryneus placed his hands palms down on the marble of the throne. His eyes narrowed. "Later, you can explain, in detail, why I would even consider giving that permission." He clapped his hands, and servants brought forward two stools. "Bring food and drink. It seems I must hear the whole of this story in order to understand why Mycenae poses an immediate danger to us. Can I at least assume that Atreus' army is not already on its way?"

"The stone that may start that avalanche is still on the road," said Melanion as he sat. "We have time for the full tale."

The king studied his elder son's face. "Begin with the day you rode north and fill in each detail so that I may understand the full extent of the mess you have landed us in."

Melanion clenched his hands, then carefully released them. This was not the time to argue who was to blame. He shared his father's frustration. His attempt to avoid battle might yet carry the conflict right to the walls of his city.

Chapter Twenty-three

Thirteenth day after the full moon

A novice led Panacea to the central sanctuary of the temple of Artemis. "I will see if the high priestess is available to see you," she said, then slipped into the shadows between the columns that lined the quiet courtyard.

The high priestess will see me. She might keep me waiting a bit to show I didn't summon her, but she'll come. A messenger from her shrine, one that normally kept to itself, was unusual enough to warrant attention. Panacea walked over to the still pool in the center of the stone-paved courtyard.

Not a breath of wind reached this haven, so the pool was perfectly still. With the sun directly above, the water shone with yellow light. In the mirror-like surface, she saw a perfect reflection of her face. She ran her fingers across her cheeks. The journey of the last half-moon had not changed her appearance, though she felt much else had shifted.

She sensed a movement in the air, heard the soft brush of bare feet on stone. She said, "I greet you, Canace, high priestess of Artemis, in the name of my father and of the Mother Eurynome."

"Eurynome? You have been wandering a bit, Panacea." The priestess came up beside her, bent to touch the surface of the water. Gentle ripples sent sparkles of reflected sunlight dancing across the columns. "Did the moon bring you?"

"My horse was already saddled when the crescent moon rose red." Panacea realized that Canace had chosen a robe the color of the moon. It was embroidered with pictures of deer, a robe usually reserved for days of high ritual. The moon's rising had disturbed this priestess as much as it had her, even though it had quickly shifted to silver-white. Panacea knew that the goddess made a promise with this sign, but it also confirmed that danger lurked in more than one place. The goddess would not write in the sky for just one reason.

"It is not an accident that you arrive the same day as this moon." The priestess spoke quietly.

"Likely not, though I do not know all the goddess sees, only my part of the hunt."

"I doubt that you are on a chase such as the Huntress Artemis usually undertakes." Canace rose, studied Panacea's face.

"True. I seek information about a northern prince, one who should serve Eurynome but who has become a pawn of Poseidon."

"This prince is in the city? I have heard of no royal visitors."

"I left while he was still in Corinth," said Panacea. "In that city, he portrayed himself as a merchant."

"For what purpose?" Canace asked.

"I can only guess. I have chased this man north and then south again, but I do not know what drives him. He seeks revenge, I know, and power, I suspect, though he does not take a straight path."

"The goddess will not intervene against another Olympian." Canace shrugged one shoulder. "But you are welcome to join me for a meal and to share your story."

"Would Artemis care if King Atreus and his city were lured from her patronage to serve Poseidon?"

Canace frowned. "Why would the God of Ocean seek allegiance in Mycenae? Our city is landlocked."

"I believe his interest is Tiryns, where there have been earthshakings," said Panacea. "The prince and even your king are pawns in Poseidon's quest for revenge. His goal is to punish Tiryns, I believe, but in the process he will use Mycenae and provide something her king has long desired."

Canace nodded. "For a port, King Atreus might risk a great deal." Then she frowned. "The goddess already shares the king's attention with her brother Apollo. Another splitting of his offerings would anger her."

"Is it possible to learn what message this prince delivers to King Atreus?" Panacea asked.

"Indeed." Canace clapped her hands. The same novice who met Panacea at the gate slipped from the shadows. "Tell Lonus that I need him to make inquiries at the gate. He is looking for a northern merchant coming to Atreus. The man is called…"

"Aphoron, from Ephyra."

"Lonus should see where he stays in the city, and then inform us."

"Yes, Priestess." The girl bowed and hurried from the sanctuary.

"Come and eat with me. I need to hear the full tale of this hunt you are on."

***

Canace shook her head in disbelief. "Poseidon opened a crack deep enough to reach Hades' kingdom! The God of the Underworld must have been furious."

"Hades raged indeed. In the end, the Earthshaker was forced to close the crack. I do not know what others on Olympus will think about Poseidon's schemes."

Lines creased Canace's brow. "Artemis will not approve when she hears he tried to force yet another young woman into his bed. Although she does not expect all women to follow her path, she will honor your effort to free the girl to make her own choice."

"What of Atreus? Where do you think his ambition leads?"

"These days, the king attends Apollo's temple more than this one. His soldiers, however, come for the blessing of the Huntress. Often. And not just for a successful hunt in the hills. I sense that they expect Atreus to send them into battle." Canace's frown deepened.

The novice entered the dining hall and bowed before

the priestess. "Lonus sent word that a man arrived at the city gates with sixty companions. He claimed to be a prince from the north. His men were taken to our barracks, and the prince is with Atreus now."

"Sixty soldiers!" Panacea said. "Then some of his men have bypassed Corinth to join him, presumably to augment Atreus' army. I need to learn what he says to the king."

"Lonus' daughter serves at the palace. Especially now that Atreus is leaning toward Apollo, it has been useful to have an ear near to the king." Canace smiled at Panacea, and then turned back to her novice. "Tell Lonus I would like him to visit his daughter, let her know we are curious about this visitor."

Panacea sighed. "Thank you, Canace. With her help, we will learn what we can." *And let it be enough to plan our response.*

***

"Panacea, waken." Canace entered the sleeping cubicle, holding a small oil lamp. "We are summoned."

Panacea sat up and pressed her fingers on her temples to push away sleep. "Atreus summons you?"

"Artemis. She waits in the sanctuary. She wants you as well."

As she followed Canace along the corridor, Panacea wondered what had brought the goddess herself to Mycenae.

In the sanctuary, Artemis stood perfectly still near the pool, which reflected one star from the pre-dawn sky. Her bow and quiver leaned against a pillar, and her short hunting tunic showed the tanned skin of her strong arms and legs. Her dark brown eyes flicked across Panacea's face, then returned to her priestess.

"The priest of Apollo has been wakened, so I thought you should be up as well," the goddess said.

Canace knelt before the deity she served. "Goddess of the Hunt, Mistress of the Bow, we are honored by your presence. How can we serve you?"

"We?" Artemis asked. "I did not think this daughter of Asclepius served any Olympian."

Panacea put a fist over her heart, "Today I bring greetings from the servants of the God of Healing and from Eurynome."

"The cloth that old woman weaves grows thin," said Artemis. "Poseidon would love to borrow the shears of the Fates and cut right through it."

"And I will prevent that if I can." Panacea stepped forward. "This night, I am concerned that he twists the fabric you weave."

"Hunts in my territory, you mean. I have seen this." Artemis reached out a hand to Canace. "Stand, and hear me. Atreus betrays the protection I provide him."

"You said the priest of Apollo has been awakened. Atreus goes there?" Panacea asked

"This ambitious king sent word to my brother's priest that he will attend that temple for blessing before the sun is two handspans in the sky."

"The king is shamed by this. He should come to you." Anger sparked in Canace's voice.

"Indeed, he should come to me before he sends his army out on this kind of hunt." Artemis looked down into the pool. "Atreus seems to think Apollo's style fits with his idea of a developing city. His soldiers know better. They will come to you for my protection before obediently going to war."

"Where will they do battle?" A fist of fear clenched around Panacea's heart.

"Tomorrow they go to Tiryns, a hunt for power and ambition—and a port."

"Melanion must be warned," said Panacea. "I'll ride for Tiryns at dawn."

"Good. I do not want the Earthshaker to succeed in this." Artemis turned to her priestess. "Canace, you will tell Atreus I do not agree to the attack. If he fails to subdue Tiryns, he will know that turning from my patronage is a mistake."

"I will attend him immediately. Perhaps he will turn from this path."

"I doubt it. He thinks he needs a port." Artemis looked away from the mirror-like water and met Panacea's eyes. "You did make the Earthshaker angry."

"I protected the virtue of a young woman," said Panacea.

"Who has gone and fallen in love after all. Aphrodite gets her way with most of them. Still, better her choice than Poseidon's coercion." Artemis turned away, and then looked back over her shoulder. "Speaking of Poseidon, he is causing a storm along the south-west coast."

"This late in spring?" Canace sounded puzzled.

"There is a fleet of ships sailing there that it seems he wants to stop. For two days now, they have not been able to leave the cove where they took shelter."

Panacea's eyes went wide. "The ships of Tiryns! They will not get home before Atreus descends on the city."

"Seems to be the Earthshaker's plan. Among others. That one is busy as a honeybee and has the sting of a scorpion."

"I owe you thanks for this news, Huntress." Panacea bowed low with both hands on her heart. A thought came to her. She did not know how Artemis would respond, but it was worth a try. "As a token of my gratitude, I would inform you of a hunt that is worthy of your skill."

"Really," Artemis' brow arched skeptically.

"Poseidon has sent an unnatural shark to plague the island of Corfu," said Panacea.

"Interesting," said Artemis. "I wonder what this has to do with the rest of the Earthshaker's plots. Be sure to tell the king in Tiryns that I am the one who is looking out for his interests." With that, Artemis lifted one hand above her head and was gone.

"I don't envy you telling Atreus that the goddess opposes this action," said Panacea

Canace bent and touched the water of the pool reverently. Ripples made the reflection of the star waver. "And I don't envy you heading into a city that will soon be under siege. What news can the northern prince have brought?"

"Aphoron may have carried news of the storm. He may also have learned what damage the earthshakings have caused," said Panacea. "I must leave before Atreus announces his intention. He may restrict movement."

"Limit the travel of servants of the gods and goddesses!" Canace shook her head sadly. "He has enough pride to do that."

"I'll not take the risk." Panacea hesitated. She wondered whether Aphoron would join the army of Atreus or head off on some other project. She bit her lip. She suspected he would want to be there when Tiryns fell, but there was no way to be sure without waiting, and that she must not do. "I must get to Tiryns today. Thank you for your help. If you need anything, ask Echidna, for she will gladly repay your assistance."

"A little dose of confidence wouldn't hurt," said Canace. "I will change and go to Atreus. I hope Tiryns stands. If Atreus succeeds in this, he may abandon the Huntress, though she has been a good guide for this city."

Because they used to see themselves as hunters. The city was changing as the power of the world shifted. "For all of us then, I race for Tiryns."

Chapter Twenty-four

Last day of the old moon

"I know the city walls have never shown a sign of stress, Saon, but humor me today." Melanion watched the frown deepen on the master mason's face. The man was not convinced an inspection was necessary. "Earthshakings have been stronger and more frequent than normal. I want to be sure the walls are what they have always been." *And I hope you can complain that it was a waste of time when we're done.*

Saon tapped his thumb on the palm of his hand. "I suppose it is an opportunity to teach the apprentices how to check for shifts and crumbled masonry in ordinary walls."

Melanion waited while the man considered. Others had already gone to their work, leaving the narrow street empty. The houses lining it were small, but the signs of the masons' skill could be seen in the extra touches. The master's shop had an arched doorway. Others had sculptures above their entries. One narrow building was three stories high, proof this builder knew his craft.

Saon crossed his arms. "I suppose you cannot share with me all the reasons for this request. If you command it, I will summon men from the repairs they work at. Otherwise, the merchant who hired us will argue."

"This is the king's command," said Melanion.

Saon nodded once. He called into the shop, and a young boy came running out. He sent the boy to summon two apprentices and his assistant, then he went into the shop and returned with two long chisels and a plumb line. "Where do I find you for the report when we are done, Prince Melanion?"

"I will accompany you," he answered. "I need to know immediately if you find a problem."

The master bowed his head. "I will lead the examination inside, and my assistant will take the exterior." He launched into a description of the method they would use.

As he listened, Melanion tried to figure out what shifts the earthshakings could cause. He also sensed that the head mason was taking this opportunity to teach the prince about the wall that protected the city. Like many of the city crafters, Saon did not think the palace dwellers knew enough about their work.

When the assistants returned, they made their way to the southern gate. The wooden doors at this narrow arch stood open with sculpted lions guarding it, staring proudly toward the ocean. One of the young men climbed to the top of the massive limestone wall with a plumb line.

Melanion put a hand on a huge rock near the gate. He looked up at the wall that stood the height of two men above him. These stones had protected his city for three generations. He understood Saon's skepticism. The two narrow gates were easily defended, and the wall seemed impregnable. No one had attacked Tiryns since its construction. *But times are shifting, and I am afraid we will see the combined hammers of Mycenae and* the *Earthshaker.*

***

The sun was near the zenith when they worked their way to the northwest corner of the wall and began moving east. No flaw in the stone construction had been found, though the two masons kept up a careful examination.

When they got to the area where a secret tunnel ran underneath the wall to a hidden spring of water, they checked with extra care. Though the tunnel ran deep underneath, Melanion had worried that this place was at risk, and the masons took this possibility seriously. They found that even here, the wall showed no sign of weakness.

The lad who ran along the top of the wall danced from the inside to the outside, lowering a plumb line every 20 paces, always with an arm raised to indicate the wall was straight. Five hundred paces farther, the lad appeared again above them, but instead of dropping the plumb line he looked back over his shoulder. He disappeared. The assistant mason frowned at the empty space.

A moment later, the boy called down from above. "Saon says to study this area extremely carefully. He found some crumbled mortar."

Melanion saw new tension in the masons as they slowed their examination of the mortar in each joint as high up as they could reach. He watched the lad drop the plumb line every two paces. He himself studied the placement of the boulders at the base. *Precisely what am I looking for?*

Then, Melanion saw the metal plumb hit the rock very near the top of the wall. The lad disappeared, presumably to report to the master. He walked over to the spot and looked up. Nothing seemed out of place.

"The mortar is damaged here." The senior mason held a handful of dust in his hand. His frown deepened.

The lad appeared again. "Saon says the rocks have shifted slightly, and the wall is now leaning inward. Only a forearm's length, but the balance has been disturbed. He has sent for the rest of our crew. They will begin at the gate and work toward us." He lowered his plumb line again.

"Can you see where the shifting began or what has caused it?" Melanion ran his hand along the wall but felt nothing. He pressed his lips together and studied the stones.

"A fault in the earth would run too deep for the eye to catch, and there is no sign of shifting in the ground here." The mason looked up. "Even a forearm's shift inward is too much. The balance of the rocks is disturbed. Another earthshaking could bring this section down."

"Surely that can't happen," said the apprentice.

The senior mason pushed his chisel between two rocks and it entered right up to the wooden handle. "With the crumbled mortar and that much lean, this section is no longer secure."

Melanion clenched his hands into fists. Did Poseidon know of this weakness? Was that why he caused the earth to shake? Whether the god knew or not, the city was in danger if the wall was as vulnerable as the mason claimed. "How far does the disturbance run?" His voice was tight and hard.

The mason watched the apprentice run his line along the wall. "There. Fifteen paces along, and the wall is straight again. It is a small area."

But large enough to let in an army if it falls. "We need to know if any other parts of the wall are damaged," Melanion said.

"I believe that is why the master sent for help." The mason did not look away from his work.

Melanion turned away from the wall. *Why here? Is there something about this spot?* He examined the wide expanse of pastureland and saw only a boy and a dozen goats on the rolling grassland. But he knew this was the place where the salt marsh was furthest from the wall. The relatively level plain would give an army room to work.

That is their advantage, so what about mine? Melanion studied the marshland. Long grass grew tall and thick where the land was wet, and shrubs crowded the rises. A large herd of deer could move unseen in the thick undergrowth. A single hill rose in the middle of the swamp just east of where he stood. Though he could not see them from this vantage point, he knew that paths were laid out in the marsh, so soldiers who knew them could pass in secret. They had been carved out of the marsh for a time like this. They could do no good, however, if the wall was breached.

Horses' hooves pounded the hard ground. A moment later, Dermios rode around the eastern corner of the wall with the black stallion following closely. He pulled up his chestnut and handed the black's reins to Melanion. The stallion stamped his foot, and Melanion rubbed the horse's nose, reassuring him that Dermios would only lead him like that if the situation were urgent.

"What is happening?" Melanion asked

"Panacea arrived. Your father wants you present when she tells her tale."

Melanion mounted, but turned back to the masons. "Tell Saon we need a report as soon as possible."

The man did not look away from the rocks. "I will send the message, but his answer will be that we need to be thorough."

Melanion watched the man who now took the job very seriously. "We need a plan for repair now," he added

Now the mason did look up. "Rebuilding this section is a major task."

"Proper rebuilding can take as long as you want. What we need is a plan that will keep it from falling today and tomorrow."

***

Melanion and Dermios strode into the hall where Gryneus sat on his throne, his eyes on Panacea. "You can catch up with the first part of her story later," the king said. "Continue."

Melanion came forward so that he could see Panacea's face. She shrugged one shoulder. Dermios came up a step behind her on the other side.

Panacea spoke of her time in Corinth, filling in the details Melanion and his father needed. "Artemis herself came and confirmed that Atreus will attack Tiryns. His army marches south before another day passes."

With narrowed eyes, Gryneus looked at his son until Melanion turned to meet his gaze. "You certainly stirred things up with Poseidon. Atreus is going to break the trading relationship we have enjoyed for two generations, even though he should know that he cannot get through these walls. At least, our fleet will return before he can get here, according to your calculations."

"Your soldiers will not arrive in time," Panacea said. "Artemis told us that a violent storm has trapped a fleet of ships on the west coast, a storm of Poseidon's making."

"And the wall is damaged, Father." Melanion turned to face his father. "We found a weakened area facing north where the pasture is wide between the wall and the swamps. The mortar has decayed, and the wall leans inward. Saon will report as soon as he is sure of the extent of the damage."

Melanion squared his shoulders to face his father's ire. "The Earthshaker has loosened the rocks of the wall that protects our city."

The king stood suddenly. "And King Atreus has been told this. Informed we are shorthanded as well, I must presume." He pressed his lips together. "I welcomed the northerner Aphoron as a guest, and I have always treated Atreus as my brother. Now this." He strode from the dais and leaned on the windowsill, looking out over his city.

"You examined the area, Melanion." His uncle Broteus stepped to the front of the dais. "What can be done?"

"Before I speak, we need to know if the wall is damaged in any other place. And I would like to closely examine the landscape at the weakened spot." Melanion watched his father.

King Gryneus looked out over his city for a long time. Finally, he turned back. "Thank you, Daughter of Asclepius, for hurrying south with this news. We will find you a room to rest and refresh yourself." He spoke softly to Panacea, but with his next words his voice became hard as granite. "I want a preliminary report from the master mason in one handspan. Melanion, you have that long to examine the land near the weakened section of wall. Tell the captain of the guard to come. We will hold a council of war." Gryneus swept from the room.

Panacea turned to Melanion. "A gracious enough welcome from your father, given how angry he must be."

"Raging, I would say from the undertones of his voice. Worried as well." Melanion watched the doorway for a moment longer. "As am I. Between them, Atreus, Aphoron, and Poseidon seek to destroy the city that I love. We must stop Mycenae."

***

"The type of mortar used by the giants is a mixture unknown to us. To date it has never crumbled, so that we have not needed to replace it. Yet in this one section of wall, the mortar has turned to this." Saon held out a handful of

157

dust to the king.

Melanion read impatience in the tightness of his father's jaw. The chief mason laid out his information as slowly as a farmer plowing a field for planting.

"So far the plumb line showed that the rest of the wall is straight, though the apprentices are still checking the east-facing wall. At the spot where the mortar crumbled, the top of the wall has moved several degrees inward. If the earth shakes again, it is possible that this section of wall will fall inward."

"Possible?" Gryneus made the single word an arrow of anger.

"I cannot know for certain, but I believe the rocks in that area of wall will continue to shift—and with the mortar crumbling, at some point it will fall."

"Why that section?" asked Lycorus, the captain of the soldiers who remained in the city.

"My partner speculates that the mortar in that section was prepared differently. This is not yet confirmed," said Saon. "When we have determined the cause more accurately, we will propose a plan for repair."

"With the army of Mycenae descending on the city tomorrow, you think that is adequate?"

Saon's eyes went wide. "Army, Sire? I had not heard that an army has been sighted."

"It has not. I have other sources of knowledge. The wall must be repaired today."

The mason raised his hands, palms toward the king. "When we do not know the extent of the damage, that is impossible."

King Gryneus' hands gripped the sides of his throne. "Anyone have a different answer?"

"With a full complement of soldiers, our men could defend a breached wall," said Broteus, "but not with the number of trained men we have." He looked at Saon. "The wall must not fall. We can recruit men of the city but they will be unused to fighting, and we barely have enough weapons to arm them."

"And we have one night to make more," said Gryneus.

"Again, I need a different answer."

"A permanent fix can wait," said Melanion. "Today, we only need to shore up the wall so that the rocks do not move further."

"You have a suggestion?" Gryneus glared at his son.

"I have seen wooden beams used to hold up unsteady houses while under repair."

Saon turned to Melanion. "I have no beams long enough nor strong enough to hold up this wall."

"The hills provide trees," said Melanion. "How many would you need?"

"I have never used buttresses that long. They would have to be huge trees." Saon looked at Melanion and apparently realized the prince was serious. He frowned at the ground; deep furrows crossed his brow. "Fresh cut as they would be, I would want a trunk three handspans wide at the narrow end. For that length of wall, at least eight trunks as long as the height of six men." He shook his head. "I do not like this kind of temporary strategy."

"And I do not like our odds if the wall falls," said the king.

"I will take charge of getting the wood," said Broteus.

"Do it now," said Gryneus. "So, Prince Melanion, the plan is to hold the Mycenaeans at bay until the fleet returns?"

"That would give Poseidon too much leverage," said Melanion. "We need to defeat them quickly."

"So far, I have been told that is not possible."

"I propose that Lycorus and I take the soldiers out into the salt marsh and get behind the invaders. We can trap them between us and the wall."

"Going outside the wall is highly unusual." The king scrutinized his son's face.

"This situation requires something surprising." said Melanion. "Recruits from the crafters and farmers can patrol the top of the wall to give the appearance of a standard defense. At the gates, we leave trained men. The rest of the regular soldiers we take into the marsh along with the strongest of the apprentices."

"We have enough trained men for this plan to work, Lycorus?" Gryneus studied his captain's face.

"Prince Melanion and I have gone over the roster, and I believe we can accomplish this. The element of surprise will be key."

The king nodded once. "Melanion, study the marsh land. I want a detailed plan of approach for the troops you take outside the wall. Send your brother to the bronze smiths and tell them we need weapons. Captain, the rest of the masters and apprentices of all crafts are at your disposal. I will send riders north to watch the road. Have the heralds announce that everyone must be inside the city walls by sunset, with their animals and all the crops they can harvest. No one leaves in the morning. We prepare for a siege."

Chapter Twenty-five

Last day of the old moon

"King Kratos asks you to join him in the hall. You are to enter even if he is occupied." The steward bowed to Thalassai. "He is receiving petitioners."

Although the steward presented the summons in a deferential manner, Thalassai did not think it was a request that she could decline. She wondered if the king wanted to challenge the decisions she had made while he slept. *I suppose he needs to re-establish his authority, in the city and with me.* She had earned the steward's respect, but the king would be harder. "I will dress accordingly," Thalassai answered, and the steward bowed again as he left.

"The robe I am wearing will do, Dorlas, but an armband and bracelet, I think." Thalassai combed her hair while she waited for the girl to bring jewelry appropriate for a public appearance.

Thalassai wondered if the king's mood had improved. He had been irritable the day before, though he insisted she eat with him. After the evening meal, he had summoned a poet and kept him reciting until late in the night. Finally, when Thalassai had yawned too obviously, he had released them both. She supposed the mood was a hangover from the sleeping spell. *I wager he feared going to sleep in case he did not waken.*

While Dorlas braided her hair, Thalassai wondered about the king's threat to shift allegiance to Poseidon. She dreaded the presence of that god and knew she could not stay in Ephyra if the king carried through with it. A lump formed in her throat. She did love Brizo, and she wanted to remain with him. She was going to have to convince the king not to turn to the Earthshaker.

Thalassai slipped into the hall and waited just inside the doorway, behind the dais. The steward stood to the left of the king, and a merchant—wealthy, she guessed, by the number of bracelets he wore—stood before him.

"I will attend to your request for copper when the emissary from Paxos returns," Kratos said.

The man bowed to the king, then saw Thalassai. He bowed to her as well before leaving. The king turned.

"Come forward," Kratos commanded. "Do not hang back just because I have returned to the throne."

Thalassai came to the front of the dais. "There is something you wanted?"

"I desire your presence," Kratos said. "My steward reported how you resolved the various disputes. You did well."

"I am relieved that you agree with my decisions."

"I would like those who seek my judgement today to see you seated at my side." He clapped his hands and a servant stepped from the shadows. "Bring a stool for the princess." He smiled at Thalassai. "Though we cannot have you sitting higher than I do, the people will see I value your wisdom."

Thalassai hesitated. She was not sure she liked this smiling Kratos any better than the irritable one. He might be more pleasant, but this felt like a test. When the servant came right back with a seat for her, she knew that this was not a sudden whim. She stepped onto the dais and sat.

Listening to the petitioners, Thalassai learned many details of the economy of Ephyra. Because her home had easy access by land and water to several cities, her people specialized more and traded for what they did not produce. She realized that the Boundary Mountains cut this valley off from the plains of Thessaly and that the towns to the north and south were less developed. As a result, Ephyra was more isolated, and the people here needed to make for themselves all the goods they required.

Twice during the morning, King Kratos invited Thalassai to contribute to the discussion. The first time had to do with the value of pottery. The king was interested in what it would be worth in her city. The second issue was a young apprentice who had neglected a dye urn so that the skeins of wool were ruined. The master wanted to break the contracted relationship and release the apprentice.

"What say you, Thalassai?" Kratos turned to her and waited.

Breaking relationships is too easy in this city, Thalassai thought. The youth seemed truly unhappy as he looked at the floor with slumped shoulders. "What work do your parents do?"

"My parents farm in the north, right at the base of the mountains. We plant vegetables and barley, and we raise goats."

Thalassai noted how the boy's shoulders lifted when he spoke of the animals. *And he spoke as if he is still part of the farm.* "How long have you been apprenticed to this cloth maker?"

"I came to the city when the river began to fail. The irrigation channels to our lands were the first to dry up because we are so far from the river. My parents were afraid they would not be able to feed our family."

"You are the oldest?" Thalassai asked. The boy nodded without raising his eyes from the floor. "And you miss the farm?"

He did look up then. "And the mountains. I grazed the goats on the high slopes where I could see the whole valley. I watched the city and imagined what it would be to live here. It is not what I expected."

Thalassai smiled gently. "You miss the animals, too." Again he nodded. "And I would guess you never let the goats wander the way your mind does when spinning. Is there another in your family who would rather make cloth than herd goats and weed gardens?"

"My middle sister is already a better spinner than I."

"And the water has returned to the channels, so there is no fear of starving." Thalassai turned to the king. "Perhaps you might allow the youth to return to the work he loves and his sister could apprentice with the weaver, if their parents agree."

Kratos watched her a moment, then turned to the weaver. "You are married?"

"Widowed, but my eldest daughter lives with me and works the loom."

"Then, I agree to this proposal. Boy, you will return to your home and tell your parents our decision. Weaver, you will accept?'

The weaver frowned. "I need the help, but I will not keep the girl if she is as distracted as this lad."

"She will be thrilled to come to the city," the boy said. "You will approve of her work."

"She will not get paid for the first season while she learns the craft. Your family will lose."

"Our parents will not be as worried now. As the princess said, the water has returned."

The master nodded. "I agree to this."

"I declare it to be so," said Kratos. "You may go."

As the boy and master left the hall, the steward stepped forward. "That was the last petitioner for today, my king."

Kratos turned to Thalassai. "You showed quite a bit of sympathy for that lad. Did you not think the master's loss should be compensated?"

Thalassai thought his voice tense, but she met his narrowed eyes. "He would lose more keeping an apprentice who wished to be elsewhere." The king nodded but did not seem satisfied. "When I first came here, I heard from those who served me how their families depended on what they earned because of the failing river. Now that the water has returned, there is renewed confidence, less need for a member of the family to work away from the farm. Not everyone is a farmer at heart, but they are the foundation for your city as they are for us all."

Kratos shook his head. "A strong city needs more than farms."

"But none of us can be strong without those who grow our food and the fibers for our clothes." An idea came to her. She took a deep breath and stood. "Come to the market with me. See for yourself how happy those who work the land are, how they trust Mother Eurynome. It will renew your confidence."

Thalassai felt as if the king's eyes pinned her in place. Though he held her gaze, she longed to move. Her toes squirmed in her sandals.

"Despite the fact that the Olympians are worshipped in your home, you would defend the goddess?" the king asked

"The goddess and the farmers," said Thalassai. "You can hear from them directly how they feel now that the river has recovered."

He got to his feet. "Eurynome also thought I had been in the palace too long. I will accompany you on a short walk through the market, but that does not mean I have changed my mind about the deadline. Poseidon will continue to plague us until we accept him or find some way to bind him."

"Or until he takes his attention elsewhere," said Thalassai. "He is known to be fickle."

King Kratos shook his head. "His interest in Ephyra has not wavered. You know well what that cost."

Thalassai shivered. Poseidon's desire for the allegiance of this valley had resulted in her kidnapping. But it had also introduced her to Brizo. "Sometimes a good end comes from an evil beginning," she said.

***

Thalassai resisted the urge to fidget as the king paced the courtyard waiting for the honor guard that would accompany them. Waiting was not comfortable, but she wanted to look confident and sure of herself. She wondered what made him so uneasy. Had it really been that long since he walked the streets of his city?

At the far side of the courtyard, soldiers drilled with practice swords. The clang of metal on metal made her think of battle, and she hoped this was as close to a fight as she would get. She thought about her brother, and wondered how his hunt for Aphoron progressed. She hoped he was far from any fighting. Thalassai sighed. Brizo faced danger head-on as he hunted the shark, and there was no way to know how his task went.

She took a deep breath. Messages about those two hunts would come eventually, and she had not been away from all the action. One of Poseidon's plans had hatched like a bird from an egg right here in the palace, leaving her with important tasks to accomplish. *I too have a story to tell when the others return.*

Thalassai stood tall, and when the king turned, she met his eyes with a smile. Kratos paused, hesitated, and then smiled slowly. The honor guard arrived in their scarlet tunics, and the king's face regained its distant, proud expression. Thalassai stepped beside him with four guards in front and four behind as they left the palace courtyard.

Many people walked the streets in the cooler air of afternoon. Servants fetched water and carried sacks of grain, running the kind of errands people avoided in the hottest part of the day. They stepped aside and bowed as best they could with the heavy burdens on their shoulders. To Thalassai, they looked afraid.

Merchants and city leaders also bowed to the king. Some greeted him with a blessing from the Mother. One called on Poseidon to give the king health and the valley prosperity.

When they had passed this man, the king turned to Thalassai. "Not all my people trust Eurynome to address the needs of our current day."

"But you can see that a great many do." Thalassai hesitated. She felt her answer sounded petulant, just contradicting his observation. She considered the man who had called on Poseidon.

"In my city there are three temples. People go to seek the guidance of the one whose interests match their specific problem. The same person may attend on Athena one day and the next make an offering to Aphrodite."

"With so many spiritual directions tugging at the people, how does your father hold the city together?"

"Loyalty to Tiryns." The answer came quickly to Thalassai. "Honor to him as well."

"Acknowledging the power of the king and the city

is enough? Would not the worship of a single god be stronger?"

Thalassai chewed her lip, thinking hard. "Loyalty to our city is not so much about power as it is a commitment to look after one another."

"Really?"

Thalassai heard sarcasm in his voice, but she continued quietly, almost speaking to herself. "Honor holds us together. Trust rather than power."

"Trust can be broken."

"My father preaches honor. All the leaders do. Breaking trust is as serious as murder, which is why he would have been as furious as volcanic fire when..." Thalassai stopped herself.

"When what?"

Thalassai hesitated but the king's look demanded she continue. "When your son Aphoron betrayed the honor of a guest and kidnapped me."

"So an outsider who does not agree with your system can tear it apart."

Thalassai pulled her thoughts away from the difficult memory of her captivity. She made herself focus on the king's comment. "And an interfering Olympian can rip the fabric of your community. In a place that leans on power, a stronger army can break the bond that holds the people together. There are strengths and possible weaknesses in whatever bonds we rely upon."

"The reach of a strong god goes beyond that of a mere human, even a king," said Kratos.

They were almost at the market, and Thalassai sensed he wanted to end the discussion. Another tendril of thought came to her though. "The strength of earth grounds us all. We are about to see the produce of a world that works as it should. I think growth is Eurynome's strength, not the kind of power we see in Olympus."

Kratos watched her face a moment. "A different kind of power? Perhaps. We will continue this discussion later." He signaled to the soldiers to step behind them. A hush fell on the market as the vendors and buyers saw the king. "Now show me who has the sweetest berries," Kratos said quietly.

"I think it would be best if you tested the produce of each." Thalassai spoke as quietly as he had. "And enjoyed them all."

"So the community is held together rather than pushed apart by pride." Kratos looked at her and shook his head. "You have interesting ideas, young princess."

Thalassai blushed, and then followed him to the first stall. Kratos accepted a sample of their lettuce and complemented the farmer. As they made their way around the market, other purchasers fell back, giving them space. Thalassai felt their hesitation, their uncertainty about the king's presence.

Whispers began to circulate through the crowd, so each seller knew as the king approached that he would accept a sample of their wares. Halfway around the circuit, an old woman held out a bowl of olives to the king.

"When you were a youth," she said, "you could eat olives from dawn until dusk."

"How do you know this?" Kratos asked.

"Do you not remember the summer your father sent you to the southern hills to work for a season in an olive orchard?" The old woman looked into the king's eyes. "You lived at a farm under the rocks we call the Hydra."

"I remember a formation that looked like a monster with many heads," said the king slowly. "My father insisted I learn what it was to be a farmer. The farmer I stayed with said that I only learned the easy tasks of weeding and watering because I was recalled to the palace at the beginning of the harvest."

"I did say that, yes. Have you learned more of the work of farming since that day?"

"You were the mistress of that farm?" Kratos smiled when the old woman nodded. "I would not have known you, though I recall that time well. It was a summer of freedom as I worked with your sons, walked the hills with them, and rested in the shadow of the rocks in the heat of mid-day." Kratos took one of the olives from the bowl. "I did not have the opportunity to stay on a farm again. My father fell ill that fall, and I became responsible for the duties of the palace."

"There is still time," the woman said. "You would be welcome at our farm any season."

King Kratos laughed. Thalassai thought she heard real humor in the king's voice for the first time since she'd met him. With her memory of him as a young man, this wise woman had reached past the crust of pride he had developed.

"Perhaps when Brizo returns, I will accept this invitation." He raised a hand, palm facing the woman. "Not to work," he said with a smile, "just to see for myself what is happening on the land."

"The Mother bless you, King of Ephyra. You will see how she blesses us all." The woman bowed low.

Kratos smiled at Thalassai. "If I did not know better, I would think you had come ahead to set this up."

"I did not need to, King Kratos," said Thalassai. "Your people know Mother Eurynome blesses their land. Your shared land."

"Well. Let us see what the rest of her blessings taste like." Kratos led the way to the next stall where berries of various kinds were displayed.

Thalassai relaxed. This visit had worked out even better than she imagined it would. The king was hearing for himself how the land had been restored, how hopeful the people were. She believed he would tour at least some of the farms when Brizo returned. Her chest constricted again. She wondered again how he fared against the monster shark and when he would return to her.

Chapter Twenty-six

Last day of the old moon

Hephaestus stirred the molten metal and watched the texture of the swirling liquid. "We are ready to coat the other side of each rudder."

"You fixed the crack in the first one?" Brizo asked.

"Timon, explain to the prince." The god did not look away from his work.

"He calls it a fissure, not a crack," said Timon. "For the second side, we won't let the metal cool as much before putting in studs, and the Smith has a plan for the fissures."

Brizo nodded. He did not need to know the details, as the Smith and his assistant seemed confident in their work.

"That smells different than your usual brew," a woman said.

Brizo turned sharply. A tall, lithe figure stood next to him. She was dressed in a short brown tunic, and tight leather boots covered her feet and calves. She had a bow and quiver slung over her shoulder.

Hephaestus continued stirring the molten metal slowly, methodically. "Since when do you pay attention to my composites, Artemis?"

The goddess looked into the urn. "Since you made arrowheads for me a year ago. They stay sharp like no other. Your touch is magic."

"Craft, not magic." Hephaestus still did not look up. "I attend to the properties of metals the way you sense the movements of your prey."

"Artemis, the Huntress?" Brizo's stood taller. "We can use your help."

"I am not here to help," the goddess said.

"Then why are you interrupting my work?" the god demanded.

"Helping," she said quietly, "would mean interfering with the activity of a god who is senior to me." A smile lifted the corners of her mouth. "But the daughter of the God of Healing aroused my curiosity." She turned to Brizo. "Tell me about the monster."

"Away from our work." Hephaestus glared at the goddess. "I need to focus."

"I could ask why *you* are challenging Poseidon." Artemis raised one eyebrow.

Hephaestus looked up. "Like you, I am here because of a task that challenges my great skill. Leave me to it." Hephaestus stirred the metal and sniffed. "And the Earthshaker paid me a visit, implying to others that I support his plans. I am not inclined to indulge him in this."

Artemis watched the Smith a moment more, then turned to Brizo. "You encountered the creature?"

"One moment more, Goddess, if I may. Hephaestus." Brizo waited, but the god did not look up. "You said plans. What else is the Earthshaker doing?"

"Good Prince, you can do nothing about the other storms he has spawned." Hephaestus looked up to meet Brizo's gaze. "The attack on Tiryns that your brother instigates is out of your reach, as was the sleep he imposed on your father, so let us focus on what we need to do here."

"He put an unnatural sleep on my father?" Brizo kept his voice as calm as he could, though his heart pounded. He had left Thalassai in the middle of a new danger. "Melanion took the task of dealing with Aphoron, but I must return home."

"To do that, you have to kill the shark." Hephaestus' face became almost gentle. "The Mother whose interference brought me here wakened your father. And your lovely princess is discovering a new level of courage and wisdom. Focus on the hunt that is yours."

Brizo took a deep breath. Hephaestus was right. Thalassai and his father were out of reach until he had dealt with the shark. The task felt even more urgent, though. He turned away from the fire and met the questioning gaze of the Huntress. "I have seen the creature twice now."

"Then tell me every detail, so we can plan our hunt."

***

The sailor who had lost his leg to the shark murmured and rolled his head when Brizo put his wrist on his forehead to check for fever. The man did not waken from his drugged sleep. Talia had found herbs in the hills to sedate him, and advised he be kept asleep for this day. Brizo watched his ashen face. He should have been able to prevent this.

He looked across at the two sailors who would sit with their companion this night. Though one was the man's brother, Brizo saw no judgement in his eyes. In fact, he had overheard men praising him for entering the water and facing down the beast. He could not let himself feel pride. When the shark was dead, perhaps then he could allow himself to think that he had done his best.

"Tell me as soon as he wakens in the morning," Brizo said. "I will assure him that the palace will find work for him when he is well enough." One of the men nodded, but the man's brother looked down. The brother would know that no other work would satisfy this companion the way sailing had. Still, even a one-legged man had family to care for, and the kingdom owed him for his service.

Brizo rose and walked to the fire. The cook handed him a bowl of savory fish stew. Hephaestus would again eat at his work. He and Timon had set themselves the task of fixing any fissures or slits in the armor in preparation for the hunt in the morning. Brizo joined the circle where Artemis lounged among his companions.

"It is a dark night," said one of the sailors, "this last of the old moon. We need a story, Brizo, to give strength to our hearts."

"A fair request," Brizo said. "I am told Artemis is an accomplished story teller."

"I will tell the first. Then, I'd like to hear a song." Artemis sat straight with legs crossed beneath her. "There's a tale

172

that has been on my mind, and you may see why by the end."

All eyes were on the goddess. *This is a good distraction,* Brizo thought.

"Such a variety of creatures and people Poseidon has sired," she began, "each one as proud as their father. The Earthshaker seems to like creatures that move the earth with each step, and has fathered several giants. Two of the most prideful, with the least reason for that pride, decided they were strong enough to take over Olympus."

Artemis shook her head. "The fools caused havoc on the foothills of the mountain, but Zeus chased them away with lightning bolts flung at their feet. Why their feet, you ask? Why did he not kill them? A wary truce exists between the brothers Hades, Poseidon, and Zeus: devastating war would erupt across the land if these three interfered directly with each other."

Brizo watched the Huntress, thinking that both she and Hephaestus walked a difficult line. They had defined their role here carefully to make it hard for Poseidon to insist they stop interfering in his plan.

"Chased from the holy mountain," Artemis continued, "pride bruised and ambition thwarted, the two giants needed to prove their strength. They chose a path too many have taken when they desired to prove their manhood. They set their minds on rape.

"These two fools chose to chase goddesses. First, they found Hera, wife of the one who had defeated them. She slipped away and retreated to a distant garden to rest in fragrant peace.

"I chanced to be hunting nearby. I heard the lecherous grumbling of their voices and understood their design. I could have slipped away like Hera, but they were intent. Someone would have crossed their path and been caught by these vicious louts." She turned to Brizo and met his gaze. "Sometimes we choose to stay and face evil for the sake of others." She turned back to the fire, watched the flames as if remembering. "I led the two down to the shore and into the water. I thought they might follow me into the depths and be drowned."

Artemis laughed. Brizo heard no mirth in her voice but rather the growl of a hunter, perhaps a lion.

"I had forgotten that sons of Poseidon do not drown," she continued. "They walked across the water as I flew over the waves. 'So be it,' I called to them. 'Chase me to ends of the earth.' Their voices rumbled with desire as they strode across the dark waters of the deep. I did not need to go as far as the ice lands or the burning heat of the desert. A nearby island held the creature I needed to tempt them.

"Such an odd race across the water. I stayed just far enough ahead to hold their interest—the sons of Poseidon are not known for their attention span. When I reached the shore of the island, I called to a creature who lived there. She would meet us at the edge of the forest. I pretended that the sands slowed my progress and let the two oafs come so close they could almost touch me. Then, I left their sight. The white hind, the deer whose hooves are bright silver, appeared just inside the trees.

"The two giants shouted their pleasure and barged into the forest to reach her. She leaped away, led them to a clearing. From opposite sides, they approached with their deadly spears. She stood absolutely still as the giants charged toward her, longing to pierce her white hide. When they were almost upon her, I pulled her from the glade, and the two giants impaled each other instead of their prey. Their fall caused the island to shake and waves to spread across the ocean. News came to Poseidon that two of his sons were gone."

"He must have been angry with you," said one of the sailors.

"How could he blame me when they impaled each other?" Artemis again looked to Brizo. "I am tired of tricking Poseidon's creatures and letting him get away without payment. I will hunt the beast with you, and then I will face the Stormbrewer."

"And if you raise the ire of Poseidon?"

"This is not a child of his, only a plot that serves his ambition." Artemis shrugged. "I also wonder if he really intended the kind of destruction that will come to pass if her brood is born. Come now, I was promised a song."

"Canus, you have a strong voice," said Brizo. "Sing a song of Ephyra for the goddess."

One of the younger men stood hesitantly, but bowed to Artemis. "The leader of my company has commanded me, and so I will bring to you a song of water. Not ocean waves, but the clear sweet water of our river."

The man sang well, but Brizo thought the goddess looked preoccupied. She watched the fire, unmoving, while others tapped their fingers to the rhythm of the music. Canus sang another song about the land and hills of their homeland. Then, he sat, and silence descended on the company. None felt they should break the reverie of the goddess.

Artemis looked up. "What about the people of Corfu? You must have a song of this island?"

One of the visitors nudged his companion. This man bowed to the goddess as Canus had and began to sing. He hesitated when he finished.

"Sing again. Your voice is sweet enough," said Artemis. "But Brizo and I must talk. Come walk with me," she said to the prince.

Brizo followed the Huntress to the water's edge, where quiet waves gently lapped against the sand. Stars glistened from horizon to horizon. Straight ahead, where the mountains of the mainland were more a shadow that a shape, the claws of the scorpion reached upward. For Brizo, this constellation that honored the creature who defeated the hunter Orion reminded all hunters of the need for humility. Humility was not one of Artemis' virtues, however. This came clear to him as he listened to the plan she had developed, a way to use two ships to their advantage.

Brizo asked two questions and watched the quiet dark water as she answered. *Her plan is possible,* he thought, *dangerous and possible.* They would rise before the sun, and as they broke their fast he would lay out the strategy to his companions. Let them sleep as peacefully as they could until then.

Chapter Twenty-seven

Day of the new moon

Dermios climbed down the ladder from the top of the wall. "The defense is set." He took a quiver of arrows from the pile the soldiers had set out. "Spears have been lashed into place so that they can be seen from the ground. From outside the walls it will look as if we are well guarded." Dermios smiled wryly. "The fact that they don't move would be a clue to an intelligent invader."

"We'll try to keep them too busy to notice." Melanion was leaving an inexperienced collection of farmers, weavers, tanners, and potters to guard the walls — with small contingents of soldiers at the gates and at the spot where the wall had weakened.

He looked over those he would soon lead out through the tunnel to the well beyond the first track of swamp. The forty trained soldiers helped the younger men, mostly apprentices and young farmers, to prepare their weapons. The men checked the balance of their spears, shouldered quivers of arrows, and tested the strings of the bows they had been given. Each attempted to look confident in the face of this extremely unconventional maneuver.

The mason's apprentice dashed toward them along the base of the wall. Out of breath, he stopped in front of Melanion. "Saon says the wall will hold."

"The buttresses are in place?" Melanion asked.

The young man nodded. He put a hand on his chest to slow the heaving of his breath. "We worked all night, used the trees that the farmers dragged in, put in more rock and mortar. Nothing should move."

"Should," said Dermios. "If only we could be sure how hard Poseidon will shake it."

Melanion pressed his lips together. Everyone knew how much was at stake and how little they could count on. "The soldiers are in place?"

"The captain says they will keep invaders off the wall." Dermios shrugged. "Guards on the ground will be ready in case of a breach."

The apprentice stood straight. "That isn't needed. Saon says the wall will hold."

"Saon has done his best, and the soldiers will do theirs. We are covering every possibility. Now, choose a weapon and take your place among the ranks." He wished he shared the young man's confidence in the hurried work. It had to withstand the first attack of the Mycenaeans for his plan to succeed.

That plan made use of the terrain around the city. A band of high land ran beside the wall, but then it sloped downward into the heavy scrub of the saltwater marshes. He would lead this troop of soldiers and young men along hidden paths between the pools and mud holes, allowing them to approach unseen from behind, while the attention of the invaders was on the wall.

Melanion remembered the solemn look on his father's face as they broke their fast together before the sun rose. He appreciated that his father had not rehashed the strategy. Over a late dinner, he had pushed hard, argued against each part, and pressed Melanion to be certain of each move. The idea of lashing the spears in place had been his father's, addressing one gap in the strategy. *At least he did not dwell on the gaps we could not address.*

***

Panacea arrived with two women and a doctor. Each carried a leather pouch of tools and herbs. She said to Melanion, "I sent healers to the place where the masons have been working, and one to each of the city gates—places where the attack could be fierce. These three and I will do

177

what we can for those who fight with you outside the wall."

Melanion nodded. It was likely that they would need the healers before the day was done. Even with the element of surprise, he did not expect to avoid battle. "Ready the troops," he said to the designated captains. The word passed quickly that it was time. Silently, with as few torches as they could get by with, they formed into lines three men wide to pass through the tunnel, with the inexperienced men in the middle line. All knew that secrecy was the most important thing.

"You could have found an easier way to get out of helping to rebuild my village, you know." Dermios rubbed the scar above his eye.

Melanion laid a hand on his companion's shoulder. "We will get back to help your people. I have promised."

"Then let us get rid of Aphoron and these Mycenaeans so we can get to it."

Melanion and Dermios led the way through the tunnel. When they reached the other end, the sky was beginning to lighten. Melanion doused the torch he carried, and as the men exited the tunnel, they did the same. He led the way through the swamp to the area near the weakened section of wall. There, the troop spread out, finding dry places behind cover to wait.

With the captain of the troop, Melanion crawled up a knoll so he could see where the road approached from the north. When the sun rose a handspan above the horizon, Dermios and one of the senior men relieved them.

Melanion descended the hill and Panacea joined him. Together they walked among the groups of men. The apprentices looked the most anxious. These were young men who expected to be tanners and potters, not soldiers, though everyone knew that in a siege, all would be called on to defend the city.

Before long, Dermios jogged between the scrub bushes to find him. "Two riders raced down the road from the north. The messengers will be with your father shortly."

Melanion climbed to where he could see the wall. The men who watched the northern road could not come directly to the hidden soldiers, so he had he devised a set of flag signals to pass on the message the watchers carried. If possible, after they had reported to his father, a messenger would come to him through the tunnel. Shortly, a green flag was raised on a pole over the wall.

"Well, the Mycenaean army is on its way," said Dermios. "So far things are going as expected."

"Have we indeed read the minds of Poseidon, Aphoron, and Atreus so precisely?" pondered Melanion.

"Simple minds are easy to read," said Dermios.

Melanion shook his head, still watching the flag.

Dermios rubbed the toe of his boot on the ground. "Agreed. Presumption is as bad as arrogance. But in truth, I trust that you and your father have covered the possibilities."

Melanion still did not look away from the flag. Having chosen a risky tactic, he needed all the information he could get. It was possible the Mycenaeans would follow a path he had not anticipated, and too much was at stake to be wrong. Before long, a man jogged up through the brush, still in his riding clothes but carrying a bow.

"The Mycenaeans will be here before the sun arrives at the zenith," the rider announced.

"They left their city yesterday, then," said Melanion.

"Must have. We spotted them crossing the high pass at dawn," said the rider.

"How many?" asked the captain.

"Enough to row twenty ships," said the rider.

"Not such a large army," said Dermios.

"Five times the number we have here," said Melanion. "Inform our troops that we follow the plan as laid out." He turned back to the rider. "You may return to the city, break your fast, and help on the walls."

"I ate before dawn," said the rider. "I can remain with the soldiers who fight beside you."

"Make sure your bow is ready, then." Melanion looked toward the northern hills. "There," he said. "The dust of marching feet."

Chapter Twenty-eight

Day of the new moon

Eurynome watched as Zeus clashed swords with Apollo. The Lord of Olympus laughed when the younger god fell back, then Apollo twirled around and Zeus had to swing his sword sideways to prevent Apollo from making contact with his leg. She could not guess who would win this game, but she also could not wait to find out. "God of Lightning and God of Prophecy, may I disturb your practice for a moment?"

The two leaned on their swords. Zeus looked her over. "What aid do you seek, old woman?"

"I bring a gift for your safekeeping," said Eurynome, "and a two-bladed warning."

"I am to thank you for such a knife?"

"I thought you always worked in fours." Apollo flung his sword upward. It turned and flashed in the sun. He caught its hilt and cut the air.

"This time it is Poseidon who works in fours." Eurynome held out the four boxes. "He again enlisted the aid of Hypnos, God of Sleep."

"Do we care whom he caught this time?" asked Apollo in a tone that suggested he was not interested, although Zeus scowled.

"I thought the Lord of Olympus had forbidden this alliance. It is a concern if they disobey you," said Eurynome.

"Mine, not yours." Zeus turned back to Apollo and raised his sword to invite the practice to continue.

"Perhaps, but perhaps he is willing to risk a great deal. He put four of the kings in the lands I walk to sleep at the same time."

"We cannot help it if you no longer maintain control in

the lands you own." Apollo raised his sword and touched the tip of Zeus'.

"I own no land," Eurynome calmed her voice and placed the four boxes on the ground. "I give you the sleep spells for safekeeping. Now for the first blade I gift you: Poseidon provided the information that leads the city of Mycenae to attack Tiryns, and the attack will fail."

Apollo frowned at her. "Mycenae owes allegiance to me and to me sister. Why would Poseidon interfere there?"

"Your priests blessed the endeavor, so you will be blamed when it fails," Eurynome said.

"Why should they fail?" Apollo asked. "It seems more likely that I will benefit from this interference if no one but you knows the Earthshaker is behind it."

"Perhaps the God of Sea and Storm plans to reveal his role later. He has been shaking the ground around Tiryns, loosening the city wall." Eurynome shrugged. "Poseidon fed information to Atreus that suggested a way to easily defeat Tiryns, but the prince of Tiryns has uncovered the same information and developed a plan to counteract the damage."

"And when the attack fails, I will be blamed, even though it was Poseidon who pushed this. Whether Atreus succeeds or fails, the Earthshaker gains." Apollo raised his hand. "This shall not be." He was gone.

"So your first blade cut into his peace of mind. A lovely gift." Zeus still leaned on his sword. "The knife has a second edge?"

"Long ago, the titan Oceanus shaped a sea monster," said Eurynome. "Because even he could not control her, he locked her in a deep ocean cavern. Recently, Poseidon found the place and released her. She now plagues the fishing folk of Corfu and prevents ships from traveling the waters."

Zeus laughed. "That seems like a blade that will cut him. He thrives on the prayers of sailors."

"The creature will soon brood, and the waters of all of Greece and beyond will be populated by these monsters. No one will sail. No one will trade except by laborious land routes. The people will shake their fists and curse the gods who are supposed to protect them."

"That fool." Zeus swung his sword as though he would slay the beast or injure Poseidon. Then he placed the point on the ground. "I cannot interfere in an action undertaken by Poseidon."

"Poseidon's ambition must be curbed. He is pushing toward every horizon in his reach. He will soon push you."

"It seems he has an arrow aimed more directly at you." Zeus met her eyes. "I cannot risk a war that could destroy Olympus and all of Greece, though I agree he has overstepped all reason this time."

Zeus picked up the four boxes and turned away. Then, with his back to the goddess, he spoke in a tone of voice that suggested he had not a care or concern imbedded in his words. "Poseidon has a temple at Sounio, south of Athens. He loves the place because it is surrounded by ocean. You might find him there."

Zeus walked slowly away from her, then looked back over his shoulder. "When the dust settles, if he is curbed, I will see to it that no more storms are brewed. For the moment." Then, the God of Lightning was gone.

Eurynome sighed. She had not really expected Zeus to step in. Still, it had been worth the visit to Olympus if Apollo was able to settle things in Tiryns. Time for her to seek out the Earthshaker.

***

Blue, blue water surrounded the cliffs on three sides. Wind gusted from the south, and waves crashed against the rocks below. Eurynome could see why this place held the usually fickle love of Poseidon.

She turned toward the north, to the shining white pillars of the god's shrine. There were no houses in sight, not even a shepherd's hut. Eurynome climbed the slope to the shrine and entered the hall. The sound of her bare feet on the polished stone floor echoed among the pillars. On a pedestal in the middle of the hall sat a huge conch shell, its surface pale pink and ivory. She picked up this object that had once been the home of a magnificent sea snail. To make a shell of this size, the creature must have been ancient when it died.

Eurynome brought the conch to her lips and blew a soft note, a lament for the creature who had made it. She took a deep breath and blew again, louder and stronger.

"You come to me as supplicant?" Poseidon spoke from behind her.

She replaced the shell. "I come to tell you that the creature you freed will soon brood."

Poseidon laughed and walked around the pedestal to study her face. "And why would that matter, old woman?"

Eurynome touched the shell gently. "It is sad when old things die, like the snail that made this. The creature you freed carries children within her who would eliminate all sea travel, but still I will be sad when Artemis kills her."

"Artemis! The Huntress interferes! This cannot be allowed." Poseidon turned his back and was gone.

"I hope I did not send you north too soon," Eurynome said quietly. She was alone again holding the beautiful shell of a long dead creature. She blew softly, and the music echoed among the pillars, an act of mourning for the dead and the one who must die for the safety of the people who sailed the ocean waves.

Chapter Twenty-nine

Day of the new moon

It seemed to take forever for the army of Mycenae to descend from the hills and approach the city. Experienced soldiers paired with the younger men to help them through the time of waiting. Melanion had stationed a runner at the tunnel in case of messages from the king, and two men on the hilltop watched for the divisions of troops. Apart from this, there was nothing to do but wait.

With Dermios beside him, Melanion crawled to the hilltop. He wanted to see for himself what happened when the army reached the city. He needed to be ready for a quick move if they had guessed wrong.

The sun was straight overhead when the Mycenaeans approached the city. One small group headed south toward the city gate; the rest came straight to the open land near the place where the wall had been weakened. A wry smile came to Melanion's lips. It seemed they had predicted correctly.

Melanion watched the invaders disperse across the open ground between the wall and the edge of the swamp. Among the last to approach was a wagon pulled by oxen and loaded with two heavy timbers the size of ship masts. A few of the Mycenaeans built cooking fires, but no one set up tents the way an army would if they expected a long siege. Then the timbers were unloaded, laid out as battering rams right where the wall had been weakened.

Among the invaders, one group of soldiers stood apart from the rest. These carried weapons but did not wear the same leather armor as the others. He wished he could get a closer look, but he thought these could be the Ephyran sailors. From this distance he could not identify Aphoron.

Shortly, the group that had gone south toward the main gate marched north along the wall. A herald carrying the standard of Mycenae led the group. Melanion guessed they had delivered an ultimatum to his father. To come north that quickly meant they had not given the king time to consider a response. He left the watchers on the hilltop and slipped down to his troops.

Melanion did not have long to wait for news of the demands the invaders had made. The runner he had left by the tunnel raced up with a messenger of the king.

The messenger knelt. "This is the message from King Gryneus." He paused, then stood to look Melanion in the eyes, his voice quiet but carrying the hard determination of the king. "Your father says, 'The Mycenaeans demanded that I open the city gate and accept the rule of Atreus. I refused. Do what you must to chase them.'"

"Let's do this." Dermios lifted his bow. "I am more than ready to be done with Aphoron."

***

Melanion signaled to the standard-bearer, who had a flag wrapped tight around a spear. A herald with a long horn joined them. With ten soldiers whose swords were drawn and ready, they crept through the thick underbrush toward the wall.

A deep thud and then another could be felt as well as heard, the pounding of wood on stone. Melanion slipped to the edge of the marsh. Twenty men worked together to rush the two massive timbers toward the wall. They were protected from spears thrown down from the wall with a portable housing that reminded him of a tortoise's shell. Other soldiers stood lined up with their swords ready.

All eyes were on the wall. No watchers looked back toward the marsh. The battering rams hit the stone again, and this time the vibration went on and on.

"Earthshaking," whispered Dermios. "Poseidon is helping them. Do we begin?"

"Wait. We want them to see that the wall does not move." Melanion prayed that Saon's workers had done their job and that the wall would indeed hold.

When the ground settled, the men rushed the battering rams toward the wall again. This time others picked up long ropes with grappling hooks attached. They threw six of these up onto the wall where they caught on the rock at the top. The defenders threw two down, but the other four held. Instead of climbing, men grabbed the ropes and pulled. Not a stone of the wall shifted.

"And?" asked Dermios.

"Now." Melanion nodded to the herald who lifted his horn to his lips and blew three short notes.

Immediately, Melanion's troops raised their bows, and a rain of arrows fell on the invaders. Screams of pain showed that some of the missiles hit their marks. The invaders raised their shields toward the wall. Another volley of arrows came down upon them.

Only then did the invaders realize the arrows came from behind them. Men turned and searched for the location of those firing, but the archers were well hidden within the swamp. A third volley struck and more of the invaders cried out. A scramble of confusion erupted as men dropped the battering rams and ropes and reached for their bows and shields.

Melanion pointed to the herald who now blew one long note, the traditional signal for a parlay. He stepped forward with the standard-bearer and his guards beside him. "Hold fire. Who speaks for Atreus?" he called.

The Mycenaean captain shouted orders and his soldiers arranged themselves in two phalanxes, one facing the wall and one facing the swamp. Between the two well-ordered bodies of soldiers, wounded men moaned. The captain marched to the front of the outward facing phalanx with his standard-bearer and ten soldiers with drawn swords. Aphoron walked behind him.

"There's the pig," said Dermios quietly.

Melanion raised his eyebrows. "Keep your eyes on him." He did not take his own off the Mycenaean captain. "What provokes this attack on my city?"

"An unusual strategy, coming outside the walls." The captain stopped twenty paces from Melanion. "You have more than this little guard I presume."

"Will you parlay?" Melanion asked.

The captain gave an order, and his guard sheathed their swords, though the army behind remained alert.

Melanion signaled to his guard to lower their swords. "One more note from the trumpeter and arrows will rain again. Bows and spears are aimed at your back from the city wall. Splitting your forces to protect front and rear weakens your position." Melanion pointed to the city wall, but the captain kept his eyes glued forward. "You expected the wall to fall. You were misled, and we will allow you to retreat. If you lay down your weapons now."

The captain shook his head. "I have more men here than I believe you could muster. Why would we pull back?"

"The wall stands. See, your own men come to tell you that there is not a crack, not a movement in the solid rock of our city wall. You were deceived."

Two men scurried up beside the captain and whispered to him. The captain scowled.

"You are caught between my army and those who arm the wall. Again I ask how you will defend both flanks." Melanion stepped forward. "The first volleys were a warning, to get your attention. The next will wipe your men from our land."

"Captain, why do you hesitate?" Aphoron stepped up beside the leader of the Mycenaean forces. "You know Atreus' orders." He glared at Melanion. "The prince blusters."

Melanion ignored Aphoron. "Captain of Mycenae, I am counting."

"And I am watching Aphoron," whispered Dermios. "Hephaestus' knife is restless in its sheath."

"Command your forces to attack, Captain," Aphoron demanded. "Take this prince captive. We can add to our spoils by demanding ransom from his father."

"This is not about such a small thing as ransom," said the

captain. "And I am in command here." He held Melanion's gaze. "I have the larger force. You are outside the walls. From my viewpoint, we have the advantage."

"Nothing is as it seems, Captain. You did not come prepared for a long siege because you were promised that the wall would fall. You were told the city did not have enough soldiers to defend her. But the wall stands firm, and your wounded attest to the sting of our defense." Melanion pointed upward. At that moment, the remaining four grappling hooks were loosened from the top of the wall and flung to the ground. "This prince deceived you for his own purposes."

"The wall seems to stand, but with the shaking of the earth, even that can change." The captain scanned the marsh behind Melanion. "Your troops do not have solid ground to stand on."

"Perhaps, but they know the paths, and your men do not. Send your soldiers into the swamp, and mine will wipe them out. Not one will escape."

"He blusters! Order your men forward." Aphoron pulled his sword and pointed it at Melanion.

Dermios pulled his knife and threw. The knife slashed the back of Aphoron's hand forcing him to drop his sword.

"He drew blood at a parlay!" Aphoron pressed down with his other hand to stop the bleeding.

"You drew a sword after accepting the call to talk." Apollo picked up the knife from the ground behind the captain's guard. "This knife enforced the truce with a very precise throw." He strode across the ground and handed Dermios the knife, hilt first. He turned to face the Mycenaean captain and Aphoron.

"Lord of Prophecy," said the captain, "we had the blessing of your priest in this endeavor."

"Based on a deception," said the god.

"I shared the information I was given," said Aphoron. "If it was false, it was not my fault."

"Lord, I believe we can defeat the troop this prince of Tiryns leads," the captain stood firm.

Apollo extended his arms, one pointing to toward each

army. "Your cities are like brothers who have not grown out of their childhood rivalry. It is time to be adults. You both have something the other needs."

Melanion thought quickly. The Mycenaeans were in a corner. Their pride might well lead them to fight rather than retreating in weakness. Apollo was right that the relationship had been beneficial, though strained. Perhaps there was a way to strengthen the tie without his city becoming a vassal.

"Perhaps it is time for a new arrangement between our cities," Melanion said. "We understand your need for a port. If you withdraw, we will remove the tariffs on goods you ship through this city, and charge only half on goods that come into our port bound for Mycenae." Melanion saw a light of interest in the captain's face. "In return, you will reduce by half the price you charge for the timber and textiles we purchase from you."

"An interesting suggestion, but I cannot commit Atreus to this agreement," said the captain.

"But I can," said Apollo. "It will be enough if the price of those goods is cut by one quarter. This is the agreement." Apollo looked at Melanion with narrowed eyes. "Do not push for more when this army stands at your wall."

Melanion held the eyes of the god. He gave one sharp nod. "My healer comes now and will deal with the men who have been injured. For free. We will feed your army this one night. Except the truce-breaker. He and his companions leave now."

"How dare you! I am the one who carried Poseidon's promise." Aphoron tried to sound strong, but his voice came across as petulant.

"A promise that failed," said Apollo. "I will not be mocked by Poseidon's schemes. I declare this agreement to be in force for one year. If Gryneus or Atreus wishes to fight it, they will be free to do so after that time."

Melanion motioned for Panacea to come forward. The Mycenaean captain gave the signal for his troops to stand down. They lowered their shields and made a path for her.

"Assist the healers," the captain said to the lieutenant at his side. "We had best not lose one soldier after this fiasco."

Panacea led the healers in among the Mycenaeans, toward the cries and groans of the wounded men. Five of Melanion's guards accompanied them.

Melanion turned to Aphoron. "If you are sighted anywhere on the land of Tiryns after sunset tonight, you will be killed."

"You can't give me orders like that."

"This one I support," said the Mycenaean captain. "You embarrassed Atreus and led my men into a futile attack. If you are found in Mycenaean land, death by arrows will result. A joint guard will see you to the border of Corinth."

"And I would hurry," said Apollo. "You had best get back to your ships before news of this failed attack travels ahead of you. Corinth might impose a fine for abusing the city's port." Apollo turned his back on the blustering Aphoron. "Now, prince of Tiryns and captain of Mycenae, shake as warriors do to seal this agreement."

"This shall be, for one year," said the captain, as he held out his arm to Melanion.

Melanion gripped the man's forearm firmly as the captain gripped his. "My father will see the benefit, as will Atreus, I believe. A shift in our relationship was already on the horizon."

The captain smiled grimly. "This day was almost a disaster." He released Melanion's arm, and turned to the guards who stood behind him. "Take your cohort to escort the Ephyrans to the border of Corinthian territory. Meet us on the road home tomorrow."

Melanion nodded to his guard. "Accompany them on the road, then return. Dermios, tell the men to stand down, and then see if Panacea needs anything. I'll report to my father." He turned back to the Mycenaean captain. "The wall remains guarded, but I will return at sunset."

Chapter Thirty

Day of the new moon

"Brizo, you have shown courage," said Apro, "but this proposal, it is madness!"

"It is a calculated risk, not insanity," said Brizo calmly, though he sensed tension in others who sat around the fire in the first pale light before dawn.

"We armored our oars and rudders for a purpose." Apro crossed his arms. "We can't use plain wood. She'll rip through it like teeth through the flesh of an olive. This plan is foolish."

"Do not challenge your captain and your prince." Artemis' voice was a deceptively smooth drawl. "It is my plan, after all. I advise silence and agreement under the circumstances."

Apro turned red. He stared at his knees but said nothing more.

"We have heard that the beast uses the same strategy on any of the boats that dare the waves." Brizo thought they were betting a lot on this information, but they had to make some assumptions. "So we let her believe we are the same as any other boat. We set one ship as the decoy with four sets of oars and the rudder with no armor. As soon as she thinks she had disabled the first ship, we slip the metal coated ones into place and chase her down from behind."

"We stay near the shore to draw her within range of the archers we place there," added Artemis, "You will be our insurance that she does not run when she discovers we do not break as easily as others did."

Brizo saw a few nods around the circle. Others ate

thoughtfully as they pondered the plan he and Artemis laid out. In the light of the flickering flames, he could not be certain he read their faces clearly, but he guessed that a few felt like Apro.

"I will force no one to join this fight," said Brizo. "If you mistrust this plan, you can serve among the crew on the shore." Brizo saw several undecided sailors bristle at the idea that they would be too afraid to follow a strategy that their captain approved. Truly though, he only wanted those who trusted the idea fully to venture out on the water. The uncommitted could hamper them.

"Apro will command the forces that remain on the shore." Brizo saw Apro look up with surprise, waited until the man nodded his agreement. "The rest of you have until the sky lightens to the color of burnished bronze to say which ship you chose to sail in, or if you will remain part of Apro's shore crew. Kobis, I cannot give you a choice, as all know you are the best archer: you remain on the shore. I will command the decoy ship. Men of Corfu, there is space for some of you in the boats, more with the shore crew." Brizo stood. "I will go stand by the ships. Come to me there if you will venture onto the water."

Half his companions jumped to their feet immediately, and the rest were only an instant behind. Brizo's heart surged with pride at the courage the men showed. In the end, with so many volunteers, they drew lots for the boats. He assigned three of the men from Corfu to each boat.

Brizo watched the men set about the last preparations for the hunt. They slid the plain wooden rudder and oars into place on the decoy ship. Apro helped stow the armored rudder and oars in the hold, ready to replace the ones they expected the shark to break. The sailor had finally accepted his role in the crew, and acknowledged Brizo's leadership. *I need to be worthy of the trust I have gained.* He met Artemis' eyes.

"The nature of the prey establishes the risk in every hunt. She sets this day's tone, not you," Artemis said. "Your courage shows your companions their path. Poets will sing of this hunt."

Brizo imagined a poet singing of his courage as he led his men out onto the water. He shook his head. Singers knew little of the true hero. They never spoke of the simple determination that one felt when the path was set and could no longer be changed.

***

Not a breeze stirred the water of the bay as the shore crew pushed the two ships into the water. As soon as they could, Brizo ordered his men to press hard on the oars, allowing their companions to retreat to the beach. All remembered how close to shore the monster had come two days earlier.

From the prow of his ship, Brizo saluted the shore crew. Apro raised his bow in return, then strode into the water until he was in above his knees. Kobis came to stand beside him. "Hold oars," Brizo ordered his men.

The second ship skimmed past, and from her place by the rudder, Artemis saluted him. He let her ship get four ship-lengths ahead before giving the order to resume rowing. Brizo sensed the tension of the men on the benches. He rolled his shoulders, working to dislodge the tightness of his body. He could not aim his spear well if he let anxiety settle in his muscles.

Brizo scanned the gentle waves for any sign of the beast's approach. All he saw was the wake of the ships and the tiny whirlpools made by each stroke of the oars. It was the kind of calm sea that could lull an unwary sailor into complacency. This day Brizo and both crews knew that somewhere under the gentle blue water, the monster lurked.

Artemis looked back and raised one arm. Heading farther from the cove would eliminate any help from the archers on shore. Instead, they would troll back and forth as if they were fishing folk who expected to race to shore at first sight of the beast. Brizo spun his hand above his head, the signal to turn.

"Where is she?" asked one of the sailors when they had the ship turned. "The one day we want her, and she keeps us waiting."

"Steady forward," said Brizo, though they would turn back again when they reached the rock cliff at the northern edge of the cove.

"There!" cried the watcher positioned beside the sailor who handled the rudder.

Brizo looked back, saw the white fin of the beast cross their wake and turn straight toward them. "Steady forward." Neither boat gave any hint the sailors noticed her approach. He watched the fin of the shark race toward them. In a moment, she was too near for him to see from the prow.

"Diving!" called the watcher.

"Even strokes," Brizo said.

A loud crack of wood breaking, and the man at the rudder was thrown aside. The watcher bent over him as he appeared to be injured.

"His arm!" cried the watcher. "Broken."

"You'll take the rudder," Brizo called.

Another crack rent the air, and the first rower at the back lurched on his bench. The end of the oar in his hand showed the beast had broken through the wood.

"Brace yourselves, but keep rowing," Brizo called as a second oar on the same side was taken.

Brizo saw the slash of the beast's tail as she dove under the ship. A moment later, her nose and fin rose in front of the boat, heading back toward them, almost within his reach. Still, he held his spear and waited. She went for the oars on the port side, and men were thrown as she ripped through the first two. She lashed the water with her tail as if to declare they were crippled and headed for the other boat.

"Now!" Brizo cried.

Immediately, the sailors grabbed the armored oars that lay in the bottom of the boat and slid them in to replace the ones that had been broken. Two sailors helped the watcher remove the damaged rudder, and replaced it with the armored one.

Brizo watched the beast's fin as she headed for the second boat. With full force, she hit the rudder. The other boat bounced in the water.

"Hard forward!" he called. In an instant, they were

moving toward the other ship. He saw the white snout of the shark break the surface of the water as she opened her mouth to break the oars of that boat. The boat swung slightly, and the men lurched on their benches, but the armor held. The rowers settled again into a regular rhythm.

Brizo pressed his lips together in a terse smile. First success. He raised his spear, saw that Artemis on the other boat had an arrow on the bowstring.

The white fin rose directly behind the other ship and drove straight toward the rudder a second time. Again the boat shivered when she struck, but held its course. Again Hephaestus' metal turned her teeth.

Brizo's boat was within two ship-lengths of the other. The shark sensed their approach and turned on them. *Now,* he thought. Artemis drew back her bowstring and shot. The arrow stuck just behind the beast's fin. In an instant, the Huntress loosed another arrow and hit the same spot. A line of red bled into the water. The shark turned with a slash of her tail.

My turn now. Brizo poised the spear behind his head. He threw with all his might, aiming for the same spot Artemis had hit. It stuck, and the line of red became a stream.

The creature thrashed and opened her mouth wide. With another arrow ready on the bowstring, Artemis shot into her mouth. The arrow stuck in the cartilage and held her mouth open. The beast lashed her tail, throwing her head one way and then the other.

She dove, but with her mouth jammed open, she could not sustain the depth. The creature surfaced but swam hard away from the ships that had damaged her.

"Bowmen!" Artemis called. "Don't lose her."

The two men strode farther into the waves. Their bows held arrows with ropes tied to them. As the beast cut across the quiet waters, leaving a streak of red behind her, the men released high arcing shots. One of them hit her on the side. Immediately, the men on the shore tightened the ropes and hauled. The beast thrashed.

"Get to her," shouted Brizo. His men rowed hard to get close to the beast. The other boat was only a length behind them. Brizo held another spear in his hand, waiting until they got close.

Three prongs of lightning struck beside his boat, and a wind hit them broadside. A figure with a trident stood on the shore behind the two archers. The figure swept his arm forward, and a wave knocked the archers off their feet. He raised his trident and wind swirled around him.

"Hold the ropes!" called Brizo.

"Don't let her go," yelled Artemis, "whatever Poseidon does."

With that, the God of Storm aimed his trident at the ship Artemis was in. A wave rose and crashed over it. The rowers strove to right the boat. When he shifted his aim to Brizo's ship, a wind swirled, spinning them around despite the efforts of the sailors. The god laughed.

"This shall not be," boomed a great voice. The form of a man rose from the waves, his huge head crowned with hair like seaweed waving in an ocean current. "The storm shall cease!" he called, and immediately the wind around Poseidon disappeared. The ocean waves calmed.

Poseidon aimed his trident at the newcomer and lightning sprang toward him. With a wave of his hand, the titan deflected it.

"To the beast," called Brizo, and his sailors got the ship back on course. An arrow sank into her back, and Brizo launched his spear to hit the same spot.

The creature thrashed her tail and threw her head from side to side. She could not dislodge the arrow in her mouth or the weapons that stuck in her back. The shore crew pulled her toward the sand. She rolled and rolled again, wrapping the rope around her.

"I've got this," Artemis said. "Hard forward," she said to her rowers. The ship surged toward to the creature. Her boat bounced in the turbulence the shark created. "Steady." Artemis waited until the shark rolled again. She shot her arrow through the softer underside of her mouth directly into her brain. The creature thrashed her tail once, then ceased to roll. "Haul her in!"

The sailors pulled hard on the rope, slowly moving the

dead weight of the beast toward the shore.

"Get to the shore," Artemis said to her rowers. "He's the titan Oceanus," she called to Brizo.

"Head in." Brizo turned again to the watch the two who faced each other on the shore. The titan's intervention had been crucial. They could not have killed the beast if Poseidon had kept the ships off balance with wind and wave.

Artemis jumped from her boat as soon as it touched the sand, and Brizo landed a moment later. He ran behind her to where the two sea gods stood with Hephaestus keeping them apart. He wondered if there would have been a violent storm between them if the third god had not been there.

"I might thank you, Poseidon, for providing such a challenging hunt if you hadn't almost sunk my boat." Artemis voice was hard as an arrowhead.

"How dare you interfere with my creature?" Poseidon pointed his trident at the goddess. "After this smith had already assisted the hunters." He glared at Hephaestus.

Hephaestus laughed. "At times I think that you are the slowest learner on Olympus, Earthshaker."

"I have been explaining to the young storm god that the creature is mine, not his." Oceanus crossed his arms. "This young one seems to have forgotten that I crafted her an age before he spun his first storm."

"You did not appreciate her worth, old man," said Poseidon.

"And you still don't appreciate the danger she presented," said Oceanus. "She was about to brood."

"Why would that concern me?" Poseidon put the butt of his trident on the ground.

"Because," said Artemis, "every one of her children would have been as vicious as she was. No one would ever have sailed the waters of Greece again."

"I would protect those who showed me allegiance." Poseidon lifted his head and folded his arms.

"I doubt that you would have controlled the mother much longer," said Oceanus, "and you would have had no leverage over her children."

"Come and see what you were about to set loose on those

who expect you to protect them." Artemis stepped back so that the god could see where the sailors had hauled the shark up onto the beach.

Eurynome had come to the beach, and she knelt beside the creature and ran a gentle hand across her side. In a moment, she stood with a baby shark as long as her forearm laid across her hands. She walked toward Poseidon. "See the teeth of this creature, just like her mother." Eurynome's voice was quiet. "There were ten of these little ones inside her, almost ready to swim on their own, six of them female. They would have bred more of their kind. The sea would never have been safe again."

Poseidon frowned at the creature Eurynome held. "That is not what I intended."

"But without the skill of these hunters, it would have been the consequence," said Eurynome. "You owe them a debt of thanks."

"What is finished is finished," Poseidon grumbled. "I will bury the creature."

"No," said Oceanus. "She was a creature of the deep and my creation. I will return her body to the ocean." The titan strode across the sand and lifted the shark in his arms. He walked away across the waves.

"We will not forget what you did for us." One of the men of Corfu knelt before Artemis.

"Thank the men from Ephyra," said the Huntress. "I just came for the fun of a good hunt."

"You can bury this last creature." Eurynome held out the dead baby shark to Poseidon. "So that you remember the devastation you would have caused."

"Don't irritate me, old woman. You already made your point." Poseidon turned away.

Eurynome lifted her eyebrows. "Irritate? You threaten the peace of this whole coast, not to mention the errand you sent Aphoron on, and you speak of irritation. Fortunately, none of your plans have ended up quite the way you intended."

"You know nothing."

"I don't think my brother is pleased with your interference in Mycenae," said Artemis. "I would avoid

Olympus for a while if I were you."

"Enough!" Poseidon raised his trident high, sending one bolt of lightning straight up, then he was gone.

"He did not even have the courtesy to bury this poor thing." Eurynome gently stroked the dead baby shark she still held.

"I will take it," said the man from Corfu, "and raise a cairn so that we do not forget who threatened our way of life and who saved it." He took the small creature with less gentleness than the goddess displayed.

"Now," said Hephaestus, "I will get Timon started on the job of re-forging plows and knives. Then, I must get back to my own work."

Brizo placed both hands over his heart and bowed to the god. "Your armor saved this hunt. Thank you also for the training you have given Timon. I doubt he'll return to sailing when we get back to Ephyra."

"I should hope not. He's as good an apprentice as I've ever trained." The Smith limped away, toward the men who were already stoking the forge fire.

Brizo turned to Eurynome. "One ship will remain here so that the men can restore the implements we melted down. Myself, I will sail for home as soon as we can remove the armor from our oars, but that cannot be until tomorrow."

"I believe I can carry news for you so that the princess and your father do not worry longer than necessary." Eurynome smiled gently.

"Thank you," said Brizo. He bowed low to Artemis. "I am honored to have hunted with you," he said. "Your aid saved this adventure."

"I did not aid you. Never say I did." Artemis put her hand on his forearm, and he gripped hers in a warriors' handshake. "I simply took up a challenge that I could not possibly resist."

"One more thing, Huntress," said Eurynome. "All Olympus would have paid the price if this plan had come to its unintended fruition. I hope that is sufficient grounds for Zeus to impose some limits on Poseidon's actions."

Artemis nodded. "My brother and I will petition Zeus

to set a punishment for the Stormbrewer. I believe he will insist that Poseidon leave the west alone for a time. Poseidon overreached himself here." Artemis was gone.

Eurynome pushed Brizo's hair off his forehead. "You did good work here. I am proud of you. Those who wait for you will be as well."

Brizo bowed his head and when he raised it, the Mother was gone. *Time to get to work.* There were tasks to be done if he hoped to return to Ephyra the next day. Brizo let himself imagine that return, victorious in the hunt. His father would be waiting, and Thalassai.

Chapter Thirty-one

Day of the new moon

The shadow of the palace wall stretched across the courtyard where Thalassai watched the soldiers of her city drill with a group of palace guards. The clang of sword on sword rang through the still air of evening, and the men shouted encouragement to one another. Thalassai had come out to lend her support to this joint exercise, though she tried not to cheer for her home city's soldiers. This practice was intended to strengthen the ties between it and her chosen city.

Asira crossed the shadowed courtyard toward her. Thalassai tried to guess at the conflicting messages she read on the priestess' face. The lines around her eyes showed concern, but there was a smile on her lips.

"A message has come through the link," Asira said. "It passed through several hands, but it originated with Panacea. There was a failed attack on your city."

"An attack on my home!" Thalassai exclaimed. "Was this Aphoron's doing?"

Asira shook her head. "I do not know. There are no details, only the news that your city is safe."

Thalassai's heart pounded. If Melanion had been injured, she thought the message would have included that, but there was no way to be certain. "We should inform the king of what you have heard."

The king was not in the throne room, and a servant informed them he was in the garden. They found him standing on the palace wall looking out toward the ocean. They climbed the wooden stairs and saw the first crescent of the new moon almost touching the water where the sun had just set. The moon was the deep red color of blood.

"At the full moon, you claimed this is the color of promise, Priestess" said King Kratos. "To me, it looks like a bowl pouring the blood of a sacrifice."

"Or the wine of celebration," offered Thalassai.

"Celebrating what?" asked the king. "My older son is traveling beyond my knowledge, and I wonder how fares the chosen one. Your betrothed."

"Blood is the color of life, and that makes it a promise," said Asira. "As for celebration, I have had news that Tiryns staved off an attack."

"Aphoron's doing?" The king looked at her with narrowed eyes, and Asira simply shook her head. "You do not know if my son caused this." With deep furrows across his forehead, Kratos turned back to the moon. "Nor can you read in this moon news of Brizo's hunt."

"The meaning of this moon is complex," said Eurynome, who leaned against the wall on the other side of the king. "It celebrates victory for Melanion and for Brizo, but it also mourns the death of the great shark even though that was necessary."

Thalassai leaned against the wall, letting relief flood into her. Both men had accomplished their missions. She heard Eurynome's regret over any loss of life, but she felt only joy.

"And the promise?" asked Asira

Eurynome's voice was quiet. "The people of Corfu promise to remember who helped them and who threatened their way of life." Her voice gained a sharp edge. "As for Poseidon, he is warned not to push his ambition so hard."

"That is a lot for one moon to say," said Kratos. "I take it my son succeeded."

"Brizo had unexpected companions, but yes, *he* succeeded," said Eurynome.

Thalassai heard the emphasis in the goddess' voice and realized the king was avoiding the question of Aphoron. "Brizo returns soon?" Thalassai asked. She swallowed hard. "I know that the king is also concerned for his other son."

"Brizo returns the day after tomorrow. He has a task or

two to finish up, and then he will bring you his full story."
Eurynome sighed. "Aphoron has not yet decided what he
will do."

Thalassai took in a long, slow breath. "And my brother,
has he decided when he will return here?"

Eurynome's smile brightened. "You want more? Look for
him when the moon is full. Until then." Eurynome laid a
hand on the princess' shoulder, then disappeared.

"I wish she had told us what happened in my city," said
Thalassai.

"The Mother has told us what we need to know," said
Asira. "Detailed stories will come to us in due time."

"I will commission poets to craft these stories into song,"
said the king, "so we remember the deeds of these heroes."

"That would be a good thing," said Asira.

Thalassai heard a note of admonishment in the priestess'
voice. This king was, in her experience, quite inclined to
forgetfulness. She turned back to the moon. "At least, Brizo is
safe."

"And successful." The king stood straight. "We will
prepare a feast for his return." He smiled slightly as he
turned to Thalassai. "And as long as Melanion brings your
father's agreement, we will prepare for your wedding to my
son and heir as soon after the full moon as possible."

Thalassai smiled back. The king had grown in the days
since he recovered. "That will bring me joy," she said.

Chapter Thirty-two

Night of the new moon

Aphoron pulled his knife and threw it into the ground at the foot of the captain from Tiryns who had escorted him from the battlefield. The man did not flinch.

"Careful," said the captain. "We outnumber your men."

"I am beyond the border." Aphoron stood tall, crossed his arms. "That is as much as your betters instructed you to do."

"Choose your words carefully," said the leader of the cohort from Mycenae. "Some of my men are angry at the embarrassment you caused us. Do not think of crossing back to harass our camp this night. We will be on guard, and we will not be merciful."

"You blustering soldiers know nothing of the revenge I can plan. It need not be tonight." Aphoron turned his back on the guards and faced his own men.

"We head for our ships," he declared to his tired, grumbling Ephyran followers. He ordered ten to spread out from the road and hunt for something for their supper.

Then, he stalked north on the road until full dark forced a stop.

At the campsite they set up for the night, he ordered a fire built. The rabbits the men had brought down were prepared for roasting, and the limited supplies they carried were shared out. The men muttered that there was not enough, but Aphoron ignored them. He claimed a large share of the scanty meal, and then sat staring into the flames. He knew the men whispered their disapproval but he ignored them. Eventually, hungry and angry, he slept.

The sun was warm and high above the trees when

Aphoron awoke. The clearing was quiet, and the fire dead. One man sat watching him.

Aphoron glared at the sailor. "Where are your companions?"

"Most have returned to the two ships we moved down the gulf. They are going home." The man rose slowly. "Three stand guard, hidden in the trees, so that I can deliver my message. We will wait half a day at the Corinthian land bridge for you, then with or without you we sail for Ephyra."

"And if I order a different destination?"

"We won't obey. You led us into a fruitless battle. We will go home and seek the king's forgiveness."

"Go home defeated and disgraced! Impossible." Aphoron opened his hands, made his voice quieter, almost pleading. "Poseidon owes us. We can seek new opportunities from him."

"We return to Mother Eurynome. She never betrayed us, and so far seems to be stronger than the Earthshaker." The man got to his feet and turned his back on the prince.

"Stop."

The man obeyed but did not turn around. "Or what? You'll throw a knife at my back? Don't forget I am guarded." The man looked back over his shoulder. "Remember, we wait only half a day."

"Don't wait at all. I am not going to that backward valley." Aphoron folded his arms and turned away from the man, listened to his retreating footsteps. He kicked at the dead fire hoping for some embers, but there were none. All right, he would head for the nearest city with a temple of Poseidon, follow the god to his sanctuary in the south if need be.

Aphoron started walking up the road. At the nearest farm he would commandeer a horse or at least a donkey. He was not going to walk all the way. It crossed his mind that Poseidon should have known he had been abandoned by his men. Perhaps the Olympian was slipping. After all, his plan to bring down the wall of Tiryns had failed miserably. It flashed through Aphoron's mind that he still had the option of heading for Corinth to take charge of the one ship remaining to him.

His stomach rumbled. The men had not left him any food at all. He'd demand sustenance from the first farmstead he came to. *I will not beg, not from miserable sailors nor from my father.* A mount and a ride to Athens was by far the best plan.

Conclusion

Day of the full moon

Three ships with the flag of Tiryns waving in the breeze approached the shore. Thalassai watched them with her heart beating quickly. She was sure Melanion would be on one of the boats. She glanced up at Brizo, who met her eyes with a smile.

"You are certain your father will give permission for our marriage," he said shyly.

"He must," she answered, though her heart fluttered. "He always said I would be free to voice my own choice. I don't suppose, however, he imagined I would choose to live so far from him."

Selene and Asira walked across the port-land to join them. "We finally get to hear what happened in Tiryns," Selene said.

"That is your brother in the prow of the lead ship?" asked Asira.

Thalassai shaded her eyes. "It is. Melanion comes!"

Dockworkers swarmed around the ships as their prows hit the beach. Melanion jumped down and ran across the packed sand to gather his sister in an embrace. Panacea followed a little more slowly.

"I am glad to see you so well," he said. After a moment he reached one hand to Brizo, who took his forearm as Melanion gripped his. "Did someone deal with the shark your brother was supposed to kill?"

"With sailors from this city, I took on that quest. We had unexpected companions in Artemis and Hephaestus." Brizo hesitated. "Do you know where my brother is now?"

"He left Tiryns in disgrace, heading for Corinth," said Panacea. She bowed to Asira, then hugged Thalassai. "We have no idea where he went from there."

Melanion shook his head, then embraced Thalassai again. "There are many stories to tell."

"Where is Dermios?" asked Selene.

"He took a ship of crafters and sailors into the gulf. On the journey south, we met the survivors of his village. He has gone to help them, and we will join him in a few days."

"The people of Dermios' home?" Thalassai shook her head. "Another story we need to hear. What about..." she did not want to finish the question in case the answer was no.

Melanion smiled broadly. "Our father blesses your choice of husband. I bring gifts for King Kratos and a plan to build the alliance between our cities."

"The king will be pleased. He is well again, you know," said Thalassai.

"I didn't know he was ill, though we heard a hint of trouble here," said Melanion. "It seems there are three stories to tell."

"I wonder," said Asira. "The goddess always works in fours."

Thalassai frowned slightly. "My betrothal could be the fourth, and the alliance that comes with it."

"The healing of Dermios' people could be the fourth," said Melanion.

"She does not usually meddle in politics," said Asira. "But marriage or the restoration of Dermios to his family? Perhaps."

Thalassai did not think the priestess was convinced. "Sometimes, the work of the goddess is hidden from us. We do not always need to know."

"Wise words." Asira smiled. "We will celebrate the gifts we see and wait to be shown the rest."

"My father announced a welcome feast as soon as your ships were sighted," said Brizo. "A poet has already crafted our hunt into a song so that I don't recognize it at all. I will tell you what really happened, Melanion, and hear your tale before it too is turned into poetry. "

"They wrote a song about me as well, if you can imagine that." Thalassai laughed. *"One moon ago, we welcomed a visitor to our city. From then until now..."* She shook her head. "I could not have imagined these days before they happened. Perhaps that is always the way, even with the heroes in the songs we love."

If you liked this book, you might like:

Moon of the Goddess by Cathy Hird
Scorpio Races by Maggie Stiefvater
Love of the Hunter by V. L. Locey
Green by Jay Lake
Gwenhwyfar by Mercedes Lackey

CPSIA information can be obtained
at www.ICGtesting.com
Printed in the USA
LVOW04s2051030116
468944LV00004B/8/P